Gendered Space
Anthology of Stories

Gendered Space Anthology of Stories

Jehanara Wasi and
Alka Tyagi

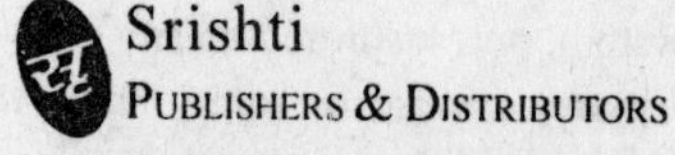

SRISHTI PUBLISHERS & DISTRIBUTORS
64-A, Adhchini
Sri Aurobindo Marg
New Delhi 110 017
srishtipublishers@yahoo.com

First published by SRISHTI PUBLISHERS & DISTRIBUTORS in 2004

ISBN 81-88575-33-X

Typeset in AGaramond 11pt. by Suresh Kumar Sharma at Srishti

Cover design by Vinayak Bhattacharya

Contents

Acknowledgements

1. Issues of Indian Literature (Sahitya Akademi)
2. Sutradhar and the author for Yatra
3. The author for A Deer in the Forest
4. The author for the Deadline

Introduction

It is an often claimed fact that life is the raw material of literature. The phrase 'raw material' however presupposes a finishing process implying that literature is a finished and refined product consisting of life elements. Literature imposes on life an order which is seemingly absent in it. Major genres of literature including drama, fiction, poetry have performed this function since their inception. Though 'verisimilitude' has been a highly desirable analytical category for literature, the sheer emphasis on this as an essential aspect brings to the fore the gap and difference that is inherent in the raw material (Life) and the finished product (Art). So with awareness of this aporia, I also wish to emphasize the 'verisimilitude' and adaptability of the genre of short fiction to bring out the most of it. Life is made up of fragments and the flexibility of the structure of a short story is just appropriate to adapt and show these life fragments while retaining a high degree of truth that is in them. Unlike the structure of a novel which tends towards a beginning of beginnings and end of all beginnings, the structure of a short story has a potential for the open endedness, which all life experiences tend to be.

The short stories in the present selection are also life-fragments which leave an enduring impact on the subject and his/her surroundings. These stories which are translated from stories written in major Indian languages not only provide a glimpse into Indian women's experience, they also indicate the fine tapestry of expression woven out of these experiences by writers writing in regional languages. The sheer variety of themes taken up in these stories disproves the prejudiced and ill-researched (but famous and well-received among English Academia) comments made by Salman Rushdie and Elizabeth West that

> "the prose writing – both fiction and non-fiction created in this period by Indian writers working in English, is proving to be a stronger and more important of work than most of what has been produced in the '16 official languages' of India, the so-called 'vernacular languages',....."
>
> [*The Vintage Book of Indian Writing* ed.. Salman Rushdie and Elizabeth West. Vintage. 1997]

Though no defence is required to argue the need for this short story collection which helps to reveal the lives of our women, it becomes all the more significant when it cuts through the hegemony of the English elitist coterie and exposes the truth of their criticism of vernacular literature in a fair light.

Although the stories in this collection are arranged in alphabetical order of names of respective languages, the whole collection can be divided into three thematic categories. The first set offers a clear view of what has always been derogatorily defined as essential female nature – woman as an angel, a subordinate, a chaste, gentle woman. But what patriarchy kept in subjugation for centuries, feminists have started celebrating those aspects of 'feminine'. The stories included in this set are 'A Girl Called Stella' by P. Lankesh; 'Didn't I Know It' by Manipadma; 'Sumati' by Hemacharya; and 'The Deadline' by Lal Singh. 'A Girl Called Stella' is a story about a dedicated young nurse who patiently serves her old whimsical patient who has been abandoned even by his sons. However in the story, the life of this old man is a sub-text of horror which gives another picture of a cruel man who prostitutes his own wife. 'Didn't I Know It' by Manipadma is about a victim of child marriage. The protagonist Sanjha becomes a widow at the age of sixteen but the maturity and dignity of her character is much beyond her years. 'Sumati' by Hemacharya is a beautiful story about an angelic little girl who comes to meet a terminally ill old man in the convent hospital and wins his heart but dies even before he could move to do something for her. 'The Deadline' by Lal Singh is another genuine piece of work revealing that aspect of human nature where relations merge into one relation of love and sacrifice. The protagonist of this story serves her dying brother-in-law in all possible roles a woman can perform – a mother, a wife, a lover. 'The Profession' by Ismat Chughtai reveals how a woman is misunderstood in the society if she doesn't fit into the prescribed roles of woman arranged for her by society.

The second set of stories are stories of rebellion by women. These stories are 'female acts', challenging the male domination when it becomes too oppressive to bear. For instance, 'Beyond the Blind Alley' by Rajee Seth, the protagonist has realised the futility of loving or expecting love from men who are capable only of lust and lechery. Her decision to abort the seed of a lecherous man is one way of resistance. However in 'Satyakaam and Jaabali' by Amitabh, Jaabali not only gives birth to the child conceived in a gang rape, she boldly brings up that child and erases the father figure completely from his life by telling him that he should put her name in the column of father as well as mother. This an other kind of resistance. 'Sometimes' by Ishwar Chander remarkably delineates a character who is highly independent, someone who is sensible enough to want love but would never stoop to beg for it. She also brings up her child without the need for a father who is in any case absent. 'Liberation' by Sujata is also a final shedding off of old slave mentality which is ingrained into our consciousness by the male society. The resounding declaration of the protagonist to her hitherto husband, "The wings you had clipped will sprout slowly. After putting the horrible past lived with you behind me, no matter whether I get back to my lost studies, or make a living by making 'appalams', I know that only golden days are ahead", is nothing short of the famous banging of the door by Nora Helmer in Ibsen's *The Doll's House.* These are grand female acts of fierce rebellion.

There is another set of stories which reveals more complex subtleties of exploitation in the Indian patriarchal set up, whether urban or rural. In 'Fish Out of Water' by Rameshwari Singh 'Kashyap', the protagonist Kunti is a victim of her stepmother's conditioned attitude in a society where marriage is the only way of life for a young woman. In the 'Saint and the Witch', Tarachand enjoyed the status of a saint while his wife was considered an ugly witch. It is only after the death of Tarachand that one gets to know about the pitiable situation of the woman who was married to a eunuch and remained a virgin all through her life. 'Let's Ask the Psychologist' by Paul Zacharia is a story that closely analyses the institution of marriage in India from the perspective of a modern educated girl who can question the one-sided approach of her parents and peers. 'The Whip' by Chandraprakash Deval is about the omnipresence and omnipotence of the exploitation of women at the hands of men. The 'Whip' becomes a metaphor for male domination and its agent that oppresses. The whip is present at all times and all spaces, it takes various forms and guises. One important and all pervading form that this whip of exploitation takes in our society is religion. 'Kokila Mahari' by Rabi Patnaik is a story about the degraded life of a Devdasi who has virtually lived like a prostitute but was ironically called the wife of Lord Jagannath, the God himself. 'The Dorsal Eye' by Himanshi Shelat is another powerful rendering of how religion and patriarchy work together to impose on woman a living condition that is nothing but inhuman.

All the stories included in this collection have women and

their experiences as subjects, except for two stories – 'Yatra' by Indira Goswami and 'Arjun' by Mahasweta Devi. These stories have been chosen because they are also 'female acts' – acts of registering an opinion. Also both the stories take the reader into a world of insurgency and politics. Incidentally both the stories show the other, the subaltern and reveal how often oppression and exploitation from the dominant class is itself the source and cause of militant insurgency. These stories are also female interjections into the political arena which hitherto had solely been considered as male territory.

Thus the stories bring out into the open the lives of Indian women – their struggles, their moves and their aspirations. And because of the virtue of verisimilitude ingrained in them, they are bound to move and bring a change to the lives of other women in a similar scenario.

Alka Tyagi
November 2, 2003.

Yatra

Indira Goswami

Professor Mirajkar and I were returning after a visit to the Kaziranga National Park. Both of us work in Delhi University, at the Department of Indian Languages, and had come to attend a conference organised by the students of Assam. We were anxious to reach Guwahati before dark. Mirajkar was not afraid of wild animals, he said, but he was definitely afraid of terrorists. One of his best friends had been killed by extremists in Punjab. He kept asking me, "Have you been able to control terrorism in this beautiful land of yours?" I really did not know what to tell him, especially since on our way we crossed quite a few checkposts where we were scrutinised and had torches shone onto our faces.

I sat in the car, looking out of the window, trying to imagine myself back on the verandah of the Kaziranga tourist lodge, listening to the wind making the thick clumps of *bijuli* bamboo rustle as if it were muga silk. I remembered the moon spotlight a huge owl that sat on a chatyan tree, its head disproportionately large, like that of a newborn baby. Mirajkar sat worrying about terrorists. Someone had told him that terrorists owing allegiance to Babbar Khalsa and the JKLF had managed to infiltrate the jungles of Assam to join local groups of extremists.

We were speeding along the National Highway. On either side were distant hills. The paddy fields were a riot of brilliant colours, flaunting gold; then, growing modest, they'd hide in Buddhist ochre, or shrink and fold into darkness. Every now and then Mirajkar would jump to alertness, as if he had imagined gunfire. Then he'd lapse into a reverie again, looking gloomily out of the window at the fields or at forests that teemed with cotton, *khaira, sisoo, holoing poma, bogi poma, bokul* and teak trees. Evening wrapped the teak in shreds of milk that the stippling sun seemed to turn magically into deer skin.

The driver broke the silence. "Last year, this road was smeared with blood. There was always crossfire of machine guns, exploding grenades. Now it's all quiet. No one is seen with a gun. Yes, no guns." ... As if a soft carpet covered it all – blood stains, the dumps of arms and ammunitions, the smell of gunpowder.

Mirajkar said, "Maybe we can't see firearms, but didn't the officer of the forest department at Kaziranga, Mr. Ahmed, say that the poachers were carrying foreign arms – 303s, 500 double barrels and 470 US carbines; that some smugglers had been caught at Mori Diphu; that two poachers were shot dead?"

Mirajkar had made a serious study of firearms and now

started telling us stories about the First World War. Ramakanta, the driver, also became eloquent with various tales of poachers from the bordering areas. He was a middle-aged man with a Nepali cap to protect his balding head from the sun. He was sturdy and short with a neck that disappeared into his shirt collar. He had small eyes, like the other Bodos of the valley, and a thin moustache. He was a good driver; he rarely used the brake or the clutch.

But my mind was elsewhere and I did not pay any attention to the talk of guns and terrorists. I was watching the forest flit past outside the car window. I saw the grand veloe trees draped in moss that grew like hair on the legs of long-tailed monkeys. There were many different trees, some with wild creepers twining themselves around trunks of *muga* silk. Some trees looked like majestic ruins dressed in shimmering gossamer. All around was monochromatic green, ranging from the richly succulent to those that remind me of *puthi*, the tiny water fish. Some leaves were round, like the heavy silver coins with Queen Victoria emblazoned on them. And the birina trees were smothered in white blossoms that looked like clouds flirting with the earth.

Mirajkar was still staring out through the window. The sound of gunfire here? No, impossible! Compared to wretched Delhi, this was heaven! Delhi, ah, who can live there any more? The bountiful Yamuna of the Afghan and Turk poets has turned into a stinking sewer. Sadar Bazar, with its teeming crowds, is a battlefield.

Gently, almost invisibly, the sun's rays turned mild, as if a huge python had shed its skin and lost itself in darkness.

... Hrr, hrr, kut, kut, krrr! The car jerked to a halt in front of a thatched shop by the wayside. Ramakanta jumped out of the car. He opened the bonnet and then came to tell us that the radiator was leaking and all the water in it had evaporated. Nothing else to do but take the car to a garage.

Mirajkar and I got off the car to walk towards two small dimly-lit shops that sold tender coconuts and tea. Mirajkar said, "It'd have been terrible if the car had broken down in the forest. Look how dark it is already." I nodded in agreement while Ramakanta paced up and down and in and out of the small roadside shops making enquiries about a garage.

All of a sudden a scrawny figure came out of a shop a little further down the National Highway. He held a kerosene lamp in his hand and wore a loose kurta and a dhoti that stopped at his knee. I couldn't make out if he wore slippers. He came up to our car and stopped. He had long hair that was tied into a low knot. He looked old and feeble. Raising the lantern, he said, "You have a breakdown? The workshop is seven miles away ... Wait, I'll stop a car for you. Driver can go and fetch a mechanic, while you please sit in my shop and have a cup of hot tea – maybe some betel-nuts, too?"

He stood right in the middle of the road swinging his lantern, his hair knot dropping loose onto his shoulders. In the flickering light, he looked ghostly.

Mirajkar and I walked into his shop. One hurricane lamp hung from a bamboo pole. Its chimney was cracked and dirty. Under a wooden bench we could see an old stove, some rusted tins. On the mud wall was a calendar with the picture of a white woman smoking a cigarette.

We sat on the bench. An old woman emerged from an inside room holding a lamp. She said, "The whole of today went by as if we were fishing at sea ... not a soul in sight."

"No customers?" I asked, surprised.

She said, "There are many shops now on both sides of the road. They know how to attract customers. They even play music!" She sidled up to me and whispered, "They sell evil stuff. But we are Bhagats. Even that picture there. My husband and I had a bitter quarrel with our children about it."

She then took a kettle and shuffled out of the room to fetch water for our tea. In the light of her lantern we could see her torn blouse. She was wearing a cotton *mekhala* and an old embroidered *chaddar* stained with betel-juice. She came back and lit the stove. It perhaps had no kerosene and soon a pungent smell filled the room.

I felt bad as I saw the old woman arranging the glasses and pouring the tea and the milk with quivering hands. "Grandma," I said, "Is there no one to help you?"

"My daughter-in-law used to, my elder son's wife. He died during the floods last year, of some unknown disease. We couldn't get any medicine for him. The doctors have turned dacoits. She was pregnant when he died and now a son's born to her. She's very weak ... can't even stand on her own feet!"

"Is there no one else?"

"I have two sons and a daughter. They used to go to school. Once. Ah, things are different now. The girl fell in love with a soldier in the Indian army which had come here to flush out the terrorists. The local boys beat her up. She's limping back to normal health ... The last seven years have been hell, daughter! The treacherous river has eaten up our land. Now there is no rice to ..."

The old man returned, still holding on to his lantern. Perhaps he had been successful in stopping a car and sending the driver to fetch a mechanic. He called out to his wife from where he stood. "Ai, mother of Nirmali, don't bore the guests with your sad tales. They're tired. Get some tea ..."

The old woman got up abruptly on seeing him. She went to him and whispered, "Manohar and some others have seen him near the railway tracks today."

The old man froze for a second. Then, "Last time too, some people said they'd seen him near the railway tracks. Don't listen to such rubbish!" he said. "Go and get the tea for our customers. They're returning from Kaziranga and must be very tired. Are there some biscuits?"

"Biscuits? All the money went into buying sugar and tea leaves last week."

Mirajkar and I cried out together, "No, no don't bother. Even black tea will do."

The old woman mumbled to herself as she prepared the tea, "God alone knows how I run this shop. Over the last seven years, the river has swallowed up so much land. That Flood Relief Committee set up their office by the roadside ... and stopped the mouths of us people with a mere one hundred rupees."

The old man shouted. "Hold your tongue, you old woman!"

She continued as if he had not spoken, "This old man feels ashamed of touching the feet of those officials who have eaten up the money sanctioned by government for flood relief. Oh! What hasn't happened to this family in the last seven years and this man struts around, his head stuffed with past glories. So what if there was a Barbarua in the family who went about with a gold-tipped walking stick and an umbrella with a silver handle, who sat on a magnificent couch ... so what? I prod him constantly yet can't get him to go and see the government officials ... and so we've been suffering for seven years ... Please tell the government about our pitiable condition. When you ..."

The old man looked angrily at her. Turning to us, he said, "Please ignore her. She starts babbling whenever she sees customers. She'd rather have tourists go and see the wretched flood-affected people who live like animals than go to Kaziranga." He glared at her. "Go, get the tea, fast. Don't forget to add crushed ginger. If there's no ginger, put in one or two cassia leaves."

It was at that moment that I caught sight of a *dotara*, hanging from the wall. I had not noticed it till then because it was behind the bench on which we sat. I was surprised to see it in the midst of other odds and ends like sacks, tins and coconut shells. The traditional two-stringed instrument had carvings on it and looked well cared for.

"Who plays this *dotara*, dada?"

A beatific smile spread on the old man's face. I couldn't have imagined a little while ago that he could smile like that. He said, "All the people visiting the Namghars on the bank of the Dipholu were familiar with this instrument of mine. Alas, the river has swallowed up many of the Namghars on its bank – Arimrah, Holapar, Kohara, Mihimukh ... people in all these places knew my *dotara*. Why, even the people Behali beyond the Brahmaputra appreciate my songs."

The old woman had finished crushing the ginger. She said peevishly, "The old man will now start bragging about the carved and mirror-studded palanquin ... The lad has been gone for two months now and might be waiting near the railway tracks, hungry and emaciated. The fossil doesn't want to hear about that!"

The old man snarled. "Shut up, you old hag. Taking eons to make two cups of tea!"

Professor Mirajkar spoke up. "I'd like to hear you play the *dotara*."

"Sure," said the old man as if he'd been waiting for just such a request. "Your mechanic will take some time to come. All those who come here for tea listen to my songs."

"Customers? No one's come for the last so many days, though so many cars went past," grumbled his wife. She turned to the old man and said, "While I give tea to the customers, go to the railway tracks with the lamp to have a look. God knows you won't get up if you sit down to gossip and to sing."

"I've heard this story before. Some months ago, didn't we hear the same rumour?" The old man mumbled as he took the two glasses from his wife and handed them over to us respectfully. Then he said in a relaxed tone, "Have your tea, please. I'll sing now."

The tea was excellent. The old man brought the *dotara*. As he started tuning it, he said, "Did you have a chance to see tigers in Kaziranga? People say there were only twenty tigers there in 1966. Now there are about sixty. Rhinos have grown from three hundred to one thousand and five hundred. There are some five hundred elephants too."

"We saw some elephants," I said. "Do they come out here also, ever?"

"Not these days because of the traffic. Before the floods they would descend on our paddy fields and all of us farmers would work together to drive them away. But tigers do come. Do you know what happened just the other day? Dimuiguria Mahanta's elephant was tied to a tree beside a roadside pond.

The elephant is very gentle. Whenever he's taken for a bath in the Dipholu, he plays with the boys and girls there. He was lying by the pond that day when a tiger jumped on him and tore away a whole chunk of flesh from his backside!"

"Oh God!" we cried out in horror. "And then?"

"Elephants are omniscient creatures. Did you know that our Moamaria revolution where the Vaishnavites fought against the Ahom kings started because of an elephant?"

"An elephant?"

"Yes. A thin and tottering elephant. It happened during the time of King Lakshminath Singha who came to the throne only in his old age. He was very friendly with his minister, Kirtinath Borbarua. Too friendly. Now, among the Ahom kings, Lakshminath and Gaurinath Singha were the most ugly. Opium eaters, they could barely keep their eyes open. Gaurinath had his eye on a fisherwoman who lived on the banks of the Dipholu. His palanquin would wait and wait outside her place while ..."

"What about the elephant?" I asked.

"Kirtinath the Borbarua had a tussle with the Moamaria mahantas. There was this law that said that mahantas must contribute elephants to the royal court as tribute every year. Once these mahantas gave an old, sick elephant to Borbarua. A mahanta went with this tottering elephant to the Borbarua. Seeing the ricketty old animal the minister turned wild with rage. He cut off the mahanta leader's ear ..."

The old woman interrupted him impatiently. "Lopping off ears indeed! Old man, for God's sake take the lamp and have a look around ... The boy might be lying somewhere, hit by military bullets."

The old man continued as if she had not spoken, "In this month of Aghan, nine thousand Moamaria soldiers made Kirtinath a prisoner while he was on his way to Rongpur. And all because of a deformed elephant, as I said!"

We sat there sipping tea and listening to the old man. Ramakantha dropped in for a while, had his tea and left. He said, "It'll take at least one and a half hours to finish the work. The mechanic has taken the radiator to the workshop."

The old woman approached me. "Only a couple of customers have come today. Dear daughter, drink one more glass of tea each. There's sugar and tea leaves."

We asked for two more cups of tea. Meanwhile, the old man was tightening the two strings of the dotara. "I barely managed to save this *dotara* from the flood. There's no one in this area who can make a *dotara* like this any more."

The old woman prodded him once more. "I'll look after the customers. Take the lamp. Go to the railway tracks. Who knows ... who knows ..."

The old man explained, "I've gone almost blind and this woman wants me to go in this darkness looking for the boy. Just the other day I fell down while I went searching for him and my knees are still aching and bruised. My heart pains too ... Listen daughter, we weren't always like this. It's the floods ... It's a pity that we had to take shelter by the side of the highway and wait for customers day after day! We were respectable people. We had two granaries, full of paddy. Even strangers were sure of a meal with scented rice and *kaoi* fish. We come from a Borbarua family who had the power to punish criminals by crushing their kneecaps. But my father was kind-hearted. If this had been daytime, I could have taken you to my house and shown you the ceremonial hat which I have managed to hold on to, his umbrella and silver vessel; a decorated couch, the silver betel-nut holder. But our paddy fields, which were as dear to me as my own flesh and blood, producing gold and pearls, are no more."

The old woman was furious. "Why are you digging up those old graves? I'll go myself to the railway tracks to see ..."

"Shut up, old woman. How many times have we heard this talk of his coming back? But nothing! He didn't come back or show his face to us. These two good people have come to my shop today. I must serve them well, make them feel comfortable." The old man started to sing a song composed by Padmapriya the Vaishnavee."

This world is futile. Like drops of water on a lotus leaf. Fate will make us a heap of ashes ... This life, this youth is all a fleeting dream ...

I could see the crisscrossing lines under his eyes. His teeth were missing, his cheeks sunken, making his nose look longer than it actually was. He sang as if the songs would never come to an end. After Padmapriya's composition, he sang several other songs from the Vaishnava saints. I felt as if I were sitting on the bank of the Dipholu, watching the moon playing in the waters.

We listened to his songs for about an hour, punctuated by his wife's restlessness. She sat muttering, "People came to say that he was seen near the railway tracks ... Even if the lad falls a prey to army bullets, he won't care ..."

Suddenly the old man stopped singing. Mirajkar hastily pulled out some money from the pocket of his coat and placed it in the betel-nut tray in front of the old man. "O mother of Nimali," the old man called out. "Keep what you charge for the tea and return the rest." Turning to Mirajkar, he said, "Why did you give so much money my dear sir? My songs are an echo of the songs of the saints. It hurts me if anyone pays me money for it. No one understands my feelings! No one!"

The old woman was staring at the money. She didn't touch it. She didn't speak.

At the moment, we heard a big bang from outside, as if a bomb had exploded! We felt as we were being thrown violently to the ground. From the shadow of a tree nearby someone emerged and walked slowly towards the shop to stand before us. Everything had happened in a fraction of a second and seeing his face now my throat went suddenly dry.

He was a young boy. Across his cheek ran a deep gash, from eye to lip – made by a bullet or a sharp knife. There was blood and pus in it. The flesh under his lips looked as if it had been ripped open and we could see his teeth in the quavering light.

I went to the old woman and took her hand in mine, gripping it tightly. We were both shivering. The boy was wearing black jeans and a khaki jacket. And what was that in his hand? A revolver? Even in a smoky light of the kerosene lamp the barrel shone. The old woman burst out in a hysterical cry,

"Oh my *kanbap*, my son! I told your father a thousand times to bring you from the railway track. Oh my son, what has happened to you? Why are you bleeding like this?" She was sobbing, her body rocking violently.

The boy didn't even look at his mother. He stared at the money lying before the old man. He pounced on it like a vulture.

The old man shouted. "This is not my money, son. Give it back to our revered customers ..."

The boy ignored his father's words. He spoke as if to himself. "Those poachers are selling a US carbine. It's an old gun, but sturdy. With this money."

He came like a cyclone. He disappeared as swiftly, a flash of lightning in the dark, still night ...

Something like a smile hovered on the old man's lips. I had never seen such a smile in my life.

... Mirajkar and I resumed our journey towards Guwahati. Neither of us spoke. It was as if we were travelling through a dark tunnel, endlessly.

This story was first published in Assamese as "Ananya Yatra" in *Sutradhar*, February 1993, Guwahati.

Arjun

Mahasweta Devi

Aghrayan was almost over and the month of Poush was just round the corner. It was not cold enough yet for the sun's warmth to be welcome.

The ripe paddy crop in Bishal Mahoto's farm had been harvested the previous day. All day, along with the harvesters and casual grain pickers, Ketu Shabar too had been collecting the leftover grains of paddy in the fields. Now, in the foggy twilight, he needed a little liquor to warm him and to relax his aching body. The desire was sure to remain ungratified, but, he told himself, there was no harm in fantasising.

His wife, Mohoni, was not with him. She came to the fields only when he was not around – Ketu was frequently in and out of jails. His offence – cleaning the jungles for the paddy crop.

It was no use trying to reason with Ketu Shabar about this. Ram Haldar gave him the job and Ketu did it. Haldar collected the profits from the felled trees, and Ketu and others like him went to jail. But what could he do? All that mattered was the four piece and the end of the day – be it for chopping down a tree or chopping up a man. In fact, it might be easier to chop up a man! Why hadn't anyone asked him to do that? Wondered Ketu. He might even earn four whole rupees that way! But he quickly corrected himself – I didn't mean it seriously, of course.

Ketu does not ever question his predicament. If you were born in the Shabar tribe of Purilia, you had to cut down the trees. And you had to go to jail. It could be no other way. If once Ketu was in jail, and something needed to be done, Halder could always find another Ketu. Nothing. Nothing lost – except that, the woman in the house had to go looking for work.

The last time Ketu had been jailed for cutting down the trees of the Forest Department, Mohini had gone out looking for work. And who knows what happened ... In spite of the inevitability of the situation, Ketu couldn't face the prospect of returning to an empty hut. No wonder the mind and the body demanded liquor. A little intoxication, a little oblivion.

Lost in reverie, Ketu was suddenly confronted by Bishal Mahato. "I have some work for you," he said.

"Is it about the votes, babu?"

"No, no! I'm not worried about that. The people will have to elect whoever I nominate, won't they?"

"Hanh, babu."

"Well? What did Ram Haldar tell you?"

"The same thing that you said."

"And what was your reply?"

"Just that I told you."

"What kind of an answer is that?"

"I am not a fool, babu," said Ketu.

"Never mind. There is something I want you to do. Are you interested?"

Ram Haldar and Bishal Mahato belonged to different parties. But for Ketu and his companions, they were two of a kind. One had to appear dumb whenever they were around. Both these deities had to be pleased, if one were to make a living in this area. But who among them would dare to say "no" to these party members? Haldar and Mahato too knew that the Shabars were indispensable – they held the world record for jail terms after all.

Now, Bishal Mahato had indeed managed to arouse Ketu's curiosity. Elections were round the corner. Bishal babu had been busy, attending meetings, giving speeches. So if the matter didn't concern votes, what could it possibly be? Whatever it was, it must be something shady.

"You have to cut down the Arjun tree," Bishal said.

"Why, babu?" Ketu was startled.

"Just do what I say."

"Please babu, I've just come out of jail, babu."

"If I wanted to send you back, would you be able to prevent it?" asked Bishal Mahato.

"No, babu."

"This is not like one of Ram Haldar's contracts. Only through his illegal operations do you land in jail. Who'd dare to arrest you if I ordered the removal of the tree from the main intersection at the Government road?"

Ketu's mind went blank. He had never thought about it, but it was true. You worked for Ram Haldar and you promptly got caught. That meant another trip to the jail. But Bishal babu's word was law. He actually ran the country, you know! So, who would send you to jail if, under his instructions, the shady tree no longer stood at the government road?

An idea flashed through Ketu's mind. "Babu, are you making a pucca road at this time, to ensure the votes?"

"Pucca road? Here? Ketu you must be mad! It has not happened in thirty years. And it won't happen now. No, I need the tree."

"A full grown tree?"

"Yes, the whole Arjun tree."

"And how would you transport it?"

"Ram babu's truck, what else."

It was as if the clear sky, the pure, cold, air and the Santoshi Ma *bhajans* blaring out on the cassette player were prompting Bishal Mahato to speak the truth.

It was that magical hour when earth bids farewell to the day and twilight disappears into the arms of night. The wind carried the smell to ripe paddy from the fields of Bandihi. But Ketu was oblivious to all that. Mohato's request had stunned him. It was as if a huge stone had been placed on his chest. This is what Chandra Santhal must have felt when, during the harvest revolution, they had pinned him down with a half-maund measure. That weight ... frightening.

Bishal Mahato and Ram Haldar belonged to two different parties. But only in word did they represent opposite camps. One conducted the Panchayat, the other ran the sawmill just outside the borders of the district. If one ordered the Arjun to be cut down, the other happily provided the transport to carry it away.

Hai! The tree couldn't be saved. It was the only surviving relic of the Bandihi jungles from the Zamindari era. It still evoked memories of the past in the minds of Ketu and his friends.

When the jungles were not jungles in name only, the Shabars had been forest-dwellers. Gone were those days when they scampered off like rabbits into its dark depths the moment they heard or saw a stranger approaching. Was that why they had been identified as Khedia Shabars, in the census records?

The elders of the tribe still revered the Arjun tree. They believed that it was a manifestation of the divine. Now Ketu was to be responsible for its death!

"Yes, babu. I'll cut it down," Ketu Shabar said. He stretched out his hand for ten rupees.

What a strange evening this was. He was even given what he had asked for.

"Go, go drink," Mahato said, "You won't be able to manage the job on your own, so get all those just released from jail. I'll see to it that you are all taken care of."

Ram Haldar's business did not stop with one or two trees. First, he put up posters, "Save the Forests," then, vandalised the jungles. Hands that wielded the axe were rewarded with torches, wrist watches, gleaming radios, cassette players, cycles, and of course, unlimited quantities of liquor. Each according to his capacity and capability. But the fallout was that whether innocent or quality, the Shabras were repeatedly prosecuted by the Forest Department of the Police.

Mahato's offer was much more promising. Who else would offer them so much?

"Very well, I'm going to the town now. For a meeting ... I must get some posters. How on earth can one conduct a campaign without wall-posters?"

"Get some for me too, babu."

"Why, do you have a wall to stick them on?"

No, no, babu. I'll spread them out on the floor when I sleep. Then I won't feel the cold in my bones."

"All right, all right. See that you cut down the tree in two or three days. I'll have it removed when I return."

"The Arjun tree, babu?"

"Yes, yes that one. Of course, it will be like the death of a mahapatra, a noble soul ...," the monkey-capped, sweater-clad Mahato muttered as he disappeared into the foggy darkness of the night.

Ketu was deep in thought. He went to look for his friends – Banamalim Diga and Pitambar – to see if they could offer a solution.

Since he was carrying liquor, they welcomed him warmly. All of them had wielded the axe. All of them were just out of jail. He who wields the axe goes to jail – that was the rule of the land. Just as it was understood that Ram Haldar would get palatial mansions built in Purulia and Bankura. That was fate. So what could they possibly do to change the order of things?

"Let me think," said Diga. Among them, Diga was treated with a little more respect. He had actually attended four whole days at the non-formal education centre! And learnt the alphabet too.

The four Shabars drowned themselves in thought and liquor. During festivals and weddings, they went around the Arjun tree, beating their *dhol-dhamsas*. After a certain wish had been granted, the tribals made the ritual sacrifice of their hair and buried it under the tree for good luck. Hadn't Diga's father said that the tree had medicinal properties?

Drunkenly, Pitamber exclaimed, "Even the Santhals come here during the Badhna Jagoran for the cow dance."

What a predicament! Cut the tree, you go to jail; don't cut

the tress, you still get jailed. What is the Shabar to do? This prosperous village of Bandihi sits where once the jungle used to be. Now it falls under the jurisdiction of the Forest Department. But of course the Shabars don't have any claim to it.

After much contemplation, Diga said, "So why should we alone take the blame? Why should only Shabars get trapped in a false case? I'm going to tell the others. After all, they too revere the Arjun. What do you say?"

Who knows how long the Arjun had stood at the intersection. No one had really noticed it all these years. It was as if the tree had been there for time eternal. But now, all of a sudden it had become enormously important for everyone. As if it was a symbol of their existence!

The Forest Department did not control only the jungles but fallow land too. So where could the Shabars go? They had simply begun to wander from place to place. Wherever they saw a gree patch of jungle land, they would settle down. Then the jungles would start disappearing. The fallow land would be sold off. Once again the Shabars would be homeless.

When the Arjun had been a young tree, the Shabars had offered prayers to it before going on hunting expeditions. Now that it was mature, how grand it was! A shiny bark, the top touching the sky. On full moon nights, the tree and moonlight seemed like one. During Chaitra and Baisakhi, its spread of leaves provided such shade. It meant so much to them. That

Arjun at the crossing.

Pitambar asked, "For how long has the Arjun been guarding us? That one tree is the entire jungle for us. And our few families, the children of the forest. Now Mohato wants that very tree?"

"What can we do? Everything belongs to Bishal babu and Ram babu."

"Till we had built our huts, we lived under the Arjun. Only later did Mohato give us the land to build our huts ..." went on Pitambar.

Diga added in his bit, "Didn't the Santhals come to it for shelter and consolation after Haldar had burnt their shanties?"

One by one, they began to recall stories about the Arjun tree. Each one realised that their lives and fate were inextricably linked with that of the Arjun. Society and the system had continually persecuted, exploited and almost obliterated this handful of tribals from the face of the earth. Now the same fate awaited the Arjun tree, the last mute symbol of their existence.

"Bishal babu is going to town. We must collect the cash from him before he leaves," said Diga.

"You will cut the trees then?"

"Five people should be enough to do the job. We'll ask for one hundred rupees, what do you say?"

"You may have to go to jail."

Frequent visits to the jail and constant exploitation by society had taught the Shabars to mask their true feelings and intentions. One face was presented to the Mahatos of the world, while the other one remained hidden. In the days of the British, the Shabars were the only ones who could be relied upon to set police stations and checkposts on fire. Today the babus were dependent on them, for these same Shabars performed the all important tasks of land encroachment, crop theft, disposal of corpses and clearing of government owned forests.

So who would be so dumb as to go to jail for cutting one single tree?

Diga gave a shrewd, cunning laugh. "You don't worry about it," he told the others. After all, he knew the alphabet, had been to the jails of district as far as Jamshedpur, Chaibasa, Medinipur and Bankura.

Bashal babu was assured that by the time he returned from the town, the job would be done. "Go and conduct your election meetings with an easy mind. Give us the money. When you come back, you'll see that the tree is not there."

"Make sure that Ram babu doesn't get a hint of what is happening."

"Why, but he'll still create a big fuss. Also, take care that no one outside the district gets news of it."

"We'll see, babu."

On the surface, politicians hoisted different flags, but underneath, they were like sugar in milk. No conflict of interest when it came down to brass tacks.

Bishal babu, you have taught the foolish Shabars many lessons haven't you – what they call non-formal education!

The leaders of the two opposite camps abuse each other at public meetings. The cadre members do not understand all this. Abuses, petty quarrels and occasional bloodshed are all part of the political system. There is bound to be some dispute over the Arjun too. But then, how many people would really support Ram Haldar? The entire village was under Bishal Mahato's sway.

A trip to the town really becomes frenzied, thought Bishal Mahato. On the way there are speeches and gatherings at the public halls and bazaars to be attended to. In the town, so many chores have to be taken care of. Get the moped light repaired, buy a new lantern, a shawl for the wife, some medicines ...

Satisfied with his trip, Bishal Mahato was returning to Bandihi. The problems of votes had been taken care of. Oh god! When would they build a proper road to the village? Nengshai, Tetka, stream after stream, and then the descent down the bamboo bridge. After that, the tortuous way through slippery paths and uneven roads.

But as he neared the village, his head reeled.

Against the backdrop of the deep blue sky, the majestic Arjun tree stood with its head held high – like a guardian of the village, keeping vigil from its lofty post. Once upon a time, this land used to be guarded by hundreds of leafy sentinels.

One by one, they have all gone, leaving no trace. Only the Arjun is left now. Alone, to guard this devastated, neglected, humiliated land of his.

Unbidden, a proverb flashed through Bishal Mahato's mind, "The leaves of the Arjun tree are like the tongue of man."

All around boomed the sounds of the *dhoti-dhamsa-damak* and the strains of the *nagra*. An agitated Bishal Mahato rushed into the village. A huge crowd had gathered around the Arjun. Its trunk was covered with *aakondo* garlands.

Haldar was standing at the perimeter of the crowd, holding on to his bicycle.

"What happened?" asked Mahato.

"The *gram-devata* has made them do it," answered Haldar.

"What? Which ill-begotten fellow says so?"

"Diga had a dream, it seems. You paid him money in the dream and instructed him to build a concrete base around the trunk. People from all the tribes – Santhal, Kehdia, Shohish, Bhumji – have now gathered to make their offerings."

"To the *gram-devata*?"

"Yes, and the crowds have not stopped coming. There is practically a mela on. We'd thought these fellows were fools. But they have made fools of us Mahato?"

Bishal stepped forward to taste the full flavour of his defeat.

What a stupendous crowd! Ketu was dancing away like a maniac, going round and round with his *dholak*.

Bishal was suddenly afraid. This tree, these people – he knew them all. He knew them very well. And yet, today, they seemed like strangers.

Fear. An uncomprehending fear gripped him.

Fish Out of Water

Rameshwari Singh 'Kashyap'

Kunti sat for a long time on the bank of the pond with her legs dangling in the water. Water got entangled in her fingers like the fibre of silk. She felt a peculiar sensation followed by a shiver in the soles of her feet which later spread through her entire flesh. Sometimes a Jhingwa fish would touch her heels and start grumbling. This made her entire body tremble. Frogs were croaking at some distance. One or two of them jumped into the water. This whipped up waves in the pond all around and disturbed the reflection of the stars in the water for a time.

This inauspicious chirping of cockroaches spread in the air. The air loaded with the fragrance of neem flowers filled the entire atmosphere.

After putting up with the unbearable heat all through the day, Kunti felt lousy. She wanted to go down to the pond and dip herself in the water. She was feeling exhausted after blowing into the earthen oven in the kitchen since evening. Her sari got stuck to her body because of the perspiration.

After feeding everyone, she somehow recharged her energy and went to the pond to fetch water for washing utensils. She knew that if various utensils were not left in the water, they would not be easily washable. Because, by the next morning when they were washed, various leftovers would become dry and stick fast to the utensils.

However, she decided not to go into the water. Making her body more relaxed, she remained sitting there.

The verandah of her house, situated on the right side, was visible from there. An earthen lamp emitted dark smoke in the outer room. She saw that the buffalo was dispersing mosquitos with its tail in the pale light of the earthen lamp. A young ox sat in one corner, ruminating. Kunti imagined that her mother was sleeping and snoring aloud. Her father might have shut his eyes exuding a raucous sound of breathlessness as he was an asthma patient. Although his eyes remained closed his breathlessness seldom allowed him to sleep soundly.

Sitva, Gitva, Motia, Gaetrea, Abhilakhva and Kaliya – must all be sleeping on the same bed. Someone's feet would be lying on another's head, whereas another's head might be hanging from the cot. And the feet of a third one might be entangled in the rope of the cot. Now she would have to arrange them on the bed properly after she got back. They would all start yelping like puppies after which her mother would roar, "This Kunti is certainly the inauspicious vamp. She likes torturing these kids. If she has her way, she would kill all of them." To this her father would add, 'Why do you make them weep? Won't you allow me to breathe? Don't you know asthma has made my life so difficult?" And if Kunti let them lie on the cot the way they were and her mother saw her, she would say, "She has a heart made of wood, nay stone. She has no sympathy for these kids. Let them die and she would remain unmoved. It is really hard to contain my anger."

Thinking about home, Kunti became sad. As though she stepped on a lump of spittle. Though she did not want it, old memories came to her mind like vivid scenes of a movie.

She was nine years old when her mother died. She remembered her death vividly. She looked like some stale brinjal. The village sorcerer burnt red, dried chilli in a pot, beat a stick on the ground and chanted *mantras* supposedly to relieve her of the ill effects of evil spirits. However, the inevitable happened. She died one day. The old women of the village howled like jackals. Her father and her uncle got their heads shaved after a few days. A massive feast was organised and within six months , her new mother arrived.

As this new mother saw her for the first time, she twitched her lips and said, "So you are my stepdaughter. Kunti had replied, "Yes." On that day her ordeal had begun. And probably no one caused her so much trouble as her stepmother did since then. She did not know what sin she had committed in her previous births so as to be compelled to live in such a hell for the past ten years.

Her new mother gave birth to a child every year. However, five of them died due to one disease or another. And the stepmother would allege that it was because of Kunti that the children died. In the meantime, her father suffered asthmatic attacks. Her stepmother also shammed illness all the time. And it was because of this habit of hers that her uncle got separated from them. Thereafter, she had to look after the children all alone. Not only had she to prepare food, she had to serve fodder and water to the buffaloes as well. Her stepmother never did any domestic chores.

For the past ten years, she had suffered from recurring headaches. But no one had time for her. Kunti remained so overworked that she did not even have time to look at her face in the mirror even once a day. Recalling all this, she felt that her body was not hers.

The moon looked like the rotten slice of a watermelon, as if entangled on top of the bamboo tree, pale, sad and shy. Due to a cloud of dust, the colour of the sky had turned dark like a slate.

Resting in the water, Kunti's feet had become benumbed. Lazily she removed her feet from the water. For some time, she thought she would fill the earthen pot with water and return home. It was already late at night. But she was overcome by a renewed feeling of exhaustion. Her whole body was aching. She took a piece of brick and started rubbing it on her heels, cleaning them.

She began brooding once again, 'I myself don't feel like sitting idle for the last three years.' As she sat down with practically nothing to do except the normal domestic chores, various kinds of ideas started troubling her mind. But what was the use of thinking about those things? Nothing was going to change. Things were going to be the same. And unfortunately only negative thoughts came to her mind. This was the only reason why she tried to remain engaged in various chores in the house. All her contemporaries were married long ago. Many of them had become mothers as well. Whenever they got together, they would start talking about their mothers-in-law and their husbands. Not only that, they exchanged various experiences with their in-laws with great interest. She did not relish such talk. But when some friend narrated her story, how could she shut her ears? And she admitted in her heart that whenever she listened to such talk, she failed to sleep a wink the following night ... She started dreaming of how her in-laws' place would be, of what nature her mother-in-law would be. Or, whether her husband would be choleric or sweet-tongued. Suddenly she would stop thinking these things with the feeling that one got only the things that one's fate decided. And she ended everything with the conclusion that however bad her in-laws' place would be, it would be certainly better than her stepmother's.

Her stepmother's words never had the warmth of a mother's. It seemed as if she was throwing firewood at her. The stepmother had completely changed the feelings of her father towards her. The year before last, her father had fixed her marriage with someone, but her stepmother put her foot down on it. She insisted that a buffalo be bought instead. There would be no cultivation on share-crop basis now, she decided. "Our own ploughs could be ploughing our fields now," she had said.

Negotiations of her marriage started once again last year. The groom was a widower and worked as a postman. Kunti's friends started teasing her. One would be calling her the owner of envelopes and postcards, while another would call her in charge of money-orders. She also felt happy in her heart. Even though the groom was a widower, at least she would now be free from the clutches of her crooked stepmother. But the stepmother played her tricks successfully once again.

She insisted that Kunti not be married off to a widower because everyone would accuse her of nurturing a grudge against her stepdaughter. And she was supposedly not ready to bear that all her life. And as Kunti's father did everything according to the wishes of her stepmother, he gave in. A good opportunity was lost.

But Kunti knew what the reality was. The fact of the matter was that her mother did not want to marry her off because she was doing the work of an ideal maid. After her marriage, it would be difficult to find a person who would look after her children properly, besides performing every domestic chore.

Something choked her throat causing her discomfort. Her

flesh and bones were throbbing with pain. She felt that her body was emitting hot steam and the veins of her head were tensed with a violent, pealing sound. She was breathing fast. She felt the hot air coming out of her nostrils above her upper lip. Her well-stuffed body was swelling and ebbing with each breath like waves of the ocean. Her lips trembled, like acacia leaves quivering in the fresh morning air.

The train on the metre gauge line crawled like little snakes moving in a single row.

The pale, moonlit night seemed to pant. Suddenly, Kunti took a long, cold breath and her entire body started shivering like the mango tree laden with flowers, during a heat wave.

There was a gorge at each step. The other day when she went to spread out wheat to dry in the sunlight on Achhaivat Singh's roof, his nephew Sunil asked her what her name was. The boy was studying at Patna. She felt like scolding and asking him why he wanted to know her name. But she controlled herself and gave him a cold stare. Seeing her mood, he went back. Similar was the behaviour of the son of Uncle Birich. Whenever she went to the pond to take a bath, he would hide in the corner of the door and gaze at her. If she gave him a good slap, he would stop becoming a Casanova. But why blame him only? Basia was no less in causing headaches to her. Wearing a silken jacket, he moved around her lane several times every day. Didn't she know his character? But he had never said anything to her. If he ever asked her anything she would give him a piece of her mind. He would never dare to come close to her again.

"These wretched people who are always on the prowl for women." If only she could tweak their ears and slap them; Kunti thought. But her major worry was how long would she be forced to undergo this torture.

Kunti felt as though some snake's poison had spread in her body. She felt suffocated as if sitting in a room filled with smoke. Every part of her body seemed to her like a separate drop of mercury. On the southern extreme of the village stray dogs were barking. On the other side, jackals were howling in the fields. In the meantime, she saw Uncle Charittar coming back after reciting prayers in the Kali temple. She heard the clatter of his wooden slippers.

Kunti thought that Uncle Charittar would not like to see her sitting on the bank of the pond at that hour. Filling her pot with water, she proceeded home.

Some distance away from her, a gourd creeper was growing on a tree. Suddenly she heard some creeping sound. She shouted, 'Who is that?' It was Bansi. He said in a light, trembling voice, "Please listen to me."

Kunti's legs and hands started quivering out of fear. She left the place at a brisk pace. She entered the outer room of her house and bolted the door from the inside. Her heart-beat was clearly audible to her. Big drops of sweat had appeared on her face. She was breathing fast. After resting for a while, she rose and put the urn in its place and cursed Bansi silently.

Her stepmother was not in the courtyard. The boys were lying criss-cross on the cot like wooden logs. An earthen lamp was burning in her father's room. The door of that room was shut. However, she heard some whisperings in the room. Her name was also mentioned in between. This made her curious about the topic of conversation. She went closer to the door without making any sound and stuck her ears there.

Her stepmother was explaining to her father, "It won't be proper to think about Kunti's marriage this year. Your asthma has come back in a bad way. Let us go to Benares for your treatment. I will also get myself checked up properly in the course of our stay there."

"This is true. But people have started pointing fingers at us. After all, how long can you keep your grown up daughter with you?" Her father countered.

"Suppose people ask you to jump into the well, would you do that? If not this year, her marriage can take place next year. She is no fish that decays if kept out of water for a long while," argued her mother.

Her father had been floored. "Yes she is not a fish that decays. Let it be the next year, then."

Kunti felt as though fifty scorpions had bitten her simultaneously. In a complete daze, she went towards her cot. But one of her feet slid into the plate with some leftovers. There was a tinkling sound. Her stepmother shouted. "What happened to you, vamp?"

Kunti felt like weeping. She wanted to overcome her shyness and tell her father that a daughter is indeed like a fish which can't remain alive for long without water. If she is kept out of it, some cat could take her away.

But she regained her composure and told her stepmother, "Nothing Mother. It was a cat. Go away! Quick Quick!"

The Dorsal Eye

Himanshi Shelat

As such the doors were not strong enough to withstand the constant, ever increasing banging and thumping. Panic-stricken and perspiring Bhanki dragged all the heavy trunks and chests close to the door and then stood in the middle of the room. Nothing more could be done now. The only way out was the window that faced Zamku's house. Bagla's father, invalid and ceaselessly coughing, might see her. That danger she could not avoid, but the old man had weak eyesight, he could not see much. Even otherwise there was no choice, either she had to run to save herself or she had to kill herself.

'Now open the door ... or we smash it ...'

'Hai, what are you waiting for? Smash it open, it won't take much time, let the witch come out ... The slut is out to destroy the whole village ... out you ...'

'Ravala, just fetch the pick axe ...'

The doors were trembling, sticks, batons, sturdy blows of fists and now a weapon more strong, deadly ...

Radki, fear lurking in her eyes, stood in a corner, mumbling;

'Night after night Bhanki has been voodooing ... Didn't I tell you long back? I knew she was after something ... every night ... you people never believed, now see for yourself what happened ...'

Bhanki's whole being clung to the door, the centre of the shack had merely her shadow. Terror seized her as she imagined what would happen when the door was smashed. In a jiffy the crowd would enter the hovel, the torrent of blows and bruises on her back, the tattered clothes, their shreds exposing her limbs ... She could see herself running breathlessly, the villagers chasing her and throwing stones at her. They were holding hot iron rods, she was helpless, she could feel streaks of blood running down from her open wounds ...

She knew there was a rope in one of the trunks. It would not take much time to make a noose. Putting it round the neck could be simple. This torture would be over within a few seconds. However, Bhanki was reluctant to do so. Deep in her heart there was someone still, perhaps Pemo, her husband, for whom she was waiting.

Otherwise, this incident had not occurred in the village for the first time. Children here died, and Gigla was one of them. That day he was playing near Bhanki's shack, there were other kids also, of Dajee and Ukad. Suddenly there was a hubbub; so the weak and aged resting in bed as well as the idlers were drawn to the spot. It appeared that Gigla had an attack of hysteria, his eyes, wide open, were cold. No vehicle was available, Bhima could get a rickshaw with great difficulty. At the Dispensary needles pierced Gigla's lifeless body. The doctor said they were too late. All this had taken place in front of Gigla's mother.

When the news of Gigla's death came to the village, Bhanki was near the fire place, watching the brown-black spots on the loaf caused by the even heat of the hearth. She knew it was not her fault, yet her legs trembled due to some unknown fear. When Pemo left the village and she did not hear from him, on seeing any one coming to her place, she used to shiver in the same way, with the same unknown fear and anxiety.

She had told Pemo not to leave for the city. Pemo, obstinate as he was, never listened to her.

'Look at Chiba's roof and walls all concrete, the city is always in need of labourers, if we get more, we may save, what is grand about staying in his wretched place?'

Possessed by this idea, Pemo repeated it and ultimately he left the village, never to return. However stories regarding him kept on reaching the villagers – stories like his death in riots or a bus accident, or his rotting in jail. Some felt that the city life offers everything, there was no need for Pemo to come to the village just because he had his wife there.

The roof, like a sieve, had been leaking during nights. The torrential rains did not let Bhanki take even a wink. Unable to decide whether to sleep or to keep awake, she would light an oil lamp and then blow it out which made. Manek and Ratan spread stories about the spooky rituals by Bhanki. Veljee, the village exorcist was now seen loitering more often as the gossips regarding Bhanki's black magic spread like wild fire.

Just then, the sudden, shocking death of Gigla –

The doors were about to break open, sticking to the wall Bhanki moved stealthily to the window. It remained closed for most of the time, so slight pushing and shoving was of no avail. Bhanki mustered up all her strength and desperately threw open the tightly shut window. It banged and cracked, for a moment Bhanki felt someone was sure to hear that, instantly she would be in the grip of that wild crowd ... But no, as her fear ebbed, she could find the whole back street quiet and deserted. Obviously, the commotion and noise were at the front door. She could jump out from the window which was not very high. She shut her eyes, thanked her stars, jumped out in haste and started running without wasting a moment.

She knew she had to run but had no idea where to go. Her legs throbbed, while panting for breath she also heard a sharp voice;

'Look at Bhanki aunt, how madly she is rushing ...'

These words to Bhanki were no less than searing blots by hot iron, they made her run even faster. The tumultuous crowd could not hear Gargi's thin voice. Bhanki ran helter-skelter to mislead and confuse the chasing crowd. This was the only sensible thing she could remember at that moment. When she could hear nothing but her stamping feet and pounding heart, she paused, half hidden by a huge pipal tree. Her bewildered eyes rivetted only in one direction. This part of the village was thinly populated, huts were scattered. Near the portico of Bhimnath Temple, somewhere around it, Dattu and Bavjee must be snoring as usual ... it was their abode. They might be dead drunk. As the thought swiftly crossed her mind, Bhanki's hand at once reached out to cover her panting, perspiring wet bosom with her sash.

Dattu had a habit. He brazenly stared at Bhanki's bosom, be it a crowded market place or a deserted narrow path. Once it so happened that at the grocer store, as she was about to take out her money from under the blouse, she saw Dattu standing behind, gazing at her intently. From that day onwards, she kept her money tied at the end of her sash. Though this did not make any difference. Dattu's eyes could almost touch her bosom and she felt terribly nervous. True, that there was no trace of lust in Dattu eyes, Bhanki had to accept, a reddish tinge could be seen, that was due to liquor, no doubt. Besides, Dattu would never utter a word, he simply stared. Otherwise he was God's good man, Bhanki knew it. The other day when she was coming from the Dispensary with her medicine, it must be Dattu who made the conductor stop the bus from her. Bhanki, busy with her morning chores might be seeking, for an opportunity to get a glimpse of Ratan's twins. Ratan would be breast-feeding them, and later the two chubby babes would play happily. Bhanki's thirsty eyes would be on the twins, while Dattu could be seen devouring Bhanki.

How soothing would it be if she could only be here a while, under this cool Pipal tree ... The soft breeze caressed her eyes and she closed them in sheer fatigue. As though talking to someone in her sleep, her lips muttered ... Dattu should be told ... protect me if you can, if you really ... Pemo was a cheat, the fellow would never die like that, he wanted to escape ... dodge ... hence all excuses ...

Bhanki's eyelids became heavier, with a jerk they opened as the powerful stampede shook her. Started, she ran straight towards Bhimnath temple, stones were hurled in her direction, sticks and axes hissed and swayed in the air.

'Finish her, don't spare her, the witch should not get away ...'

'Come here you sorceress, don't try to hide. Let us show our stuff, we are still alive to protect the village, do you understand?' 'Hai you fellas, come on, quick, double up, the witch would cheat us by changing herself into something else ... they are capable of doing such things, you see ...'

Bhanki's hair almost covered her face, the long tresses were fluttering in the air. Totally careless about her clothes, she did not bother to cover her breasts, even the black blue birthmark on her left breast was quite visible. She stood before Dattu thus, bereft of words. On seeing her in this condition, Dattu too was utterly confused, so shocked he was that he came to his senses at once, but did not know what to do. Breathless and exhausted, Bhanki could just steady herself. By then Dattu was already swept away by the commotion and shouts.

'O hoi Datta, Catch hold of that witch ...'

'Dattu is a drunkard, he is not himself ...'

'Dattu, thrash her ...'

'Dattu don't let her go, she is out to devour the males of the village ... the slut ...'

Bhanki wanted to say a lot, but Dattu, as though scared, kept falling back, his hands were groping for something, perhaps for his staff, or at least that was what Bhanki felt. Dattu lost sight of her bare breasts, looming in front of him. He was looking here and there, nervously.

'Dattu, don't you waste time, why are you standing there?'

Before Dattu could do anything, fear overpowered Bhanki and she leapt over the portico and flew like an arrow. Her strong lithe legs didn't seem to touch the ground.

'Look, the witch runs so fast that she has left us men behind ...'

Jumping into the river could be better than falling into their hands ... Bhanki's desperate decision made her choose the uneven, hilly path. There were stones and thorny bushes, she tumbled and fell down, her legs, as though broken, refused to carry her. Helpless and miserable, she lay there, melting in perspiration, her face touching the rough surface.

The violent mob and its piercing noise were drawing ever

closer. Someone dragged her, she clung to the firmly rooted grass, her clothes were in shreds, her back bare and many sticks, fists, kicks, abuses, stones weighed on it ... Then they fell on her with full might.

As she was swooning and sinking, a passing thought ... just a passing thought –

... Pimps and pigs, be you infested with worms ...

Dattu can never be in this midst ... had he not been drunk poor fellow would have helped me ... a real man in the lot ...

People do believe that a witch has a dorsal eye. All rubbish, otherwise Bhanki could have seen the mountain of a man, that strong and sturdy Dattu among the crowd.

Beyond the Blind Alley

Rajee Seth

While at work she would often sense that creepy, insect-crawling feeling on her back and her skin would tighten as if covered with water-filled sores.

Is this it? Is this why she started life anew? Left Surjit behind. For this same living ... tirelessly feeding small portions of herself to this entrenched domesticity... waiting until sundown, waiting and holding out the remains of her time for someone else.

And Surjit was one who did not resist, oppose nor did he stake a claim. He had simply said, "If you don't want to live here, don't. I won't die without you."

Yet her boss Misra had warned, "He is cunning. Later he will create a scene and refuse you a divorce." But that moment never came. Even as she had shouted and screamed accusations, Surjit was silent. On the day of the hearing the judgement was ex-parte. He never came. There was no anxiety. The silence was undisturbed by any sound of his footsteps. She felt that everything that had happened was for herself, from herself. There was nothing in it for anyone called Surjit.

If their relationship had been so one-sided, why did she have a dilemma at all?

Conscious of Surjit's brute indifference, perhaps she would never have asked for a divorce, but Misra had been adamant – freedom is essential. Legal protection! Legitimate rights! He was loath to tolerate Surjit's interference in his future. Despicable creature!

Now she wonders why she came here. Why did she choose this particular kind of life?

There she cooked and cleaned and here the servants slave. Surjit's habits were of one kind and Misra's another. He ate noisily and this one snores through his sleep. One liked red shoes, the other black. That one drank milk and this one prefers coffee. He drank Indian whisky and Misra guzzles Scotch. One man reached for her body with his kind of lust and this one claims her with another.

At night, after the lights are out, the soft mattresses on Misra's bed are very real but she fails to distinguish them from the discomfort of sleeping on the coarse cot in Surjit's house. It was only the night which freed her from the cloying snare that had become this room. In the dark she was no longer a part of it.

At midnight when Misra awakens from his snores and with feverish urgency fumbles for her on the bed, stumbling under the weight of his own body – he is no longer Misra. He becomes the same – what he thinks of Surjit – despicable creature!

When he sat before her in the office in his suit, tie, sparkling shoes and cigar he seemed to epitomise the seductive charm of upper class affectations. But at home he was stripped bare. All that was left was the banal aftertaste of this sticky truth.

She wondered whether her attraction for him was merely a reaction to his sophisticated veneer. Now freed from it why could she not see Misra as before? When he sat opposite her in the office? Why doesn't her world sway as it did once at the sight of him? To the extent that she never used to want to return home to Surjit!

Perhaps such a major decision would never have been possible if Surjit had only resisted or if Misra had not provided an option. Bribed her every day with the promise of a better life. Warmed her body with a new attraction. He had found many ways of convincing her that living with Surjit, or for that matter with anyone (to underline his scrupulous objectivity) unwillingly, is a promise of violence.

Why had he assumed that she was living with Surjit unwillingly? Perhaps because Surjit had not opposed, fought or pleaded for her. Granting her an easy, convenient release, he had moved on.

If only her freedom had not been so facile, perhaps getting Misra would have meant something, an achievement. Misra desired her so he got her. Surjit did not so he abandoned her.

What of her own desire?

These questions are disquieting now, these feelings are so alien. Sometimes while she works around the house she feels she is a minute, inconsequential part of the house.

Suddenly it feels that a large part of the house is locked away in its cupboards and boxes along with the memories of Misra's dead wife. Most of this house is spent, it is history. And Misra's wrinkled body is testimony to this wasting away. That buried past – the largest part of this house – is no part of her. But she can see it now standing in Misra's kitchen and not when she was typing in his office.

She feels it here now when every kitchen in her life will continue to be linked to Surjit's kitchen. When Misra is in his office he does not seem like Surjit, when he comes home he is Surjit!

And when Misra and Surjit become one then Surjit endears. He has no wrinkled past pasted to his arms. So what if his hand had struck her face? He would abuse her, beat her and hurl dishes. In a fit of stubbornness he would refuse to let her visit her mother and if she cried his violent possessiveness would destroy that moment.

Tired and broken she would arrive at the office and Misra would begin his ministrations. The pink-patterned porcelain teacups would soothe her wounds. And after sipping her tea diffidently when she rose to return to work, his tightening grip on her hand would pinch the cheap silver band on her finger and a tiny scream would rise in her. He would release her hand only to touch her foot with his; "I understand your needs."

What needs! This was hardly a relationship where she had the courage to ask this question. Instead she would lower her eyes and sit in silence.

He would insist that she sit closer to him. Moving away from that frontal position did help her cope with her helplessness in facing him. She was never sure what kind of confrontation she feared. Facing Misra or facing herself, reflected as she was, clearly in the pupils of his eyes.

His hands would slowly grow insistent. And after a while, he would whisper hoarsely: "Let's go out this evening... can you?"

Her quiet struggle over an answer he would decide in his favour and insist, "Call Surjit now. It won't be right to call him later."

Call Surjit? He was not like Misra with two or three telephones on his desk. He had to be traced from the workshop of the technical section. And he would come to the Supervisor's table with soiled hands and ask with extreme irritation; "Why do you bother me with trivia? If you can't come home early, is there anything I can do about it?"

At first she used to tolerate the irritation. Then she began to avoid calling him. Instead she would tell Misra that it was not important to call Surjit. Misra was relieved. From this state of not – so – important' Surjit gradually became unimportant.

She began to return home at all hours. Surjit too was staying away all night often. Now he just stayed away for longer periods. When she had asked her brother-in-law Taru she was told mockingly; "Don't you count the money in his pocket every day? You are very innocent Bhabhi."

Misra had egged her to tell Surjit plainly that she did not want to live with him any more. Surjit retorted, "If you don't want to live here any more, don't. Do you think I am going to die without you?'

No provocation, anger, abuses, violence! Nothing. If he had done so he would have perhaps exercised a right. He had freed her so easily that she felt that she must have been living out on the street all along. Had this been her home, its walls would have surely trembled to see her go.

So coming to Misra was no achievement for her. At the office she would suddenly feel that Surjit might call. But the telephone bells were only ringing in her head. Outside there was only the silence.

Misra had taken her to Mumbai soon after. Not only had he cast off the experience which was Surjit but he had wrapped her in new experiences. And she was submerged like a broken sea-shell embedded in the sand, overpowered by the rising waves but lying there unabsorbed, untouched. How odd! She was seeing the ocean for the first time. And with it she sensed immediately the suffocation of being buried under its intemperate, unrelenting force.

They had stayed in a fancy hotel. Then came the expensive clothes, the movies, the sightseeing and ... the flimsy lace gown ... he had seen and possessed her body with a passion in which even as they drowned she would pale each time at the sight of the tired wrinkled face which betrayed his wanton past. A deep sadness and that clammy feeling would linger. And her anguish like that of a wave torn from its ocean, would dog her for a long time.

When they returned, he began to insist that a legal divorce was necessary. She too agreed it was necessary. Legally too she must know to whom she belongs. They sent a notice – Surjit is an alcoholic, licentious, violent and lives off a woman's earnings.

But the stolid Surjit who faced the metal and the cacophony of his machines every day was unmoved by the outburst. He tore the notice, spat on it and said, "You can go to hell and so can your boss."

Misra was a good friend of Judge Saxena. One day forcing her to wear clothes she would even normally resent, he introduced her to the Judge adding with seasoned nonchalance, "Friend, hurry this case up, will you? You know how that damn Surjit has been harassing us."

Having had every reason to harass Misra, Surjit had merely spat on his face.

Though the divorce decree was won simply, Misra had made

it his weapon. He would tease her constantly, fiendishly, "What a struggle it was to win you darling."

If only! If only that had been true. If only Surjit had let her go with a struggle and Misra had won her with an effort, she would have had some sense of herself. Instead here she was! Bent and broken by an easy surrender to a faithless compromise! It would have been good to resist. To fight off this temptation! Fighting would have given her a sense of being!

The agony has now deepened. Since the hour that she resigned from the office and chose to face Misra's past, captive in his cupboards, since then she no longer belonged to her own present.

His desire for her which was first fanned by the furtive shadows of the hotels, restaurants and office ante rooms would consume her in its delirium. Now there is only the lifeless monotony of satiation. She winces at the realisation that she is now just like his whisky peg; a part of his evening routine.

And trapped in the daily chores of his house, she suddenly senses that insect-crawling across her back!

What if she had continued to do this for Surjit?

What if she continues to do all this for him now?

All at once she longed to return to Surjit's house. This very evening to sit in front of the coal stove in his kitchen, brew tea on its smoky glow and wait for Surjit. Her head resting on her knees, she stared at the door for a few moments anxiously awaiting the sound of footsteps. If Surjit should come and ...

She started out of her thoughts scared. The joy of reunion? With Surjit? No! No! Surjit never looks back. Neither in the past, nor towards the future. He cannot be threatened. His is a lone path, distinct from all others. When her father had died, he had dismissed her melancholia in his brusque manner, "Go stay with your mother for a few days. Come back when you are consoled."

"What if it had been your father?"

"Forget about my father," he had thundered, cutting her off as he strode out gnashing his teeth. The man who had abandoned his mother in her youth to take off with some doped sadhus aroused little sympathy in Surjit. His mother had toiled over her machine to make him worth this much. And this self-worth he carried with a vengeance. There was nothing in between. And between them?

Between her and Surjit now lie the miles of these one-and-a-half years. An eternity! History!

The history of her surrender to that looming wave that was Misra. To her own vulnerability. And the legal abyss between them called a divorce.

Misra's seed! Inside her, kicking the walls of her womb. Real and binding. And Surjit, unrelenting, aloof. There are no calls. There is no way back from here.

No paths lead into the future. Ahead lies the boundary of the graveyard which is now her future – decaying like the numerous pasts which lie buried within Misra. No paths lead anywhere from here!

If there are feet then linked to them is that inescapable helplessness of trudging on. Blocked paths lie in front and behind her ... blind alleys – winding, misty, unending.

For what has she been breaking herself? And expectations.. like bubbles of soap – arresting, colourful, endearing, momentary. And somewhere while she was chasing these bubbles, she lost her own strength to fight. Now there are only blind alleys at both ends and caught between them is a bewildered present.

She shoves aside Misra's half unbuttoned shirt and stumbles towards his room.

In the burning afternoon heat, the closed cool dark ambience of the room was pleasing. Walking towards the bed her hands reached out for the air-conditioner switch and stopped. Suddenly she turned to those heavy, imposing, rarely opened curtains. Brushed them aside. Pushed open the doors and windows.

A gust of hot air and light poured into the unfamiliar room.

Burning and blinding. Damning the conditioned order of the room. Shattering its artificial laws.

She gasped. Breaking the authority of the room filled her with joy. Just as if a sudden burst of joy cutting through pained, oppressed moments can draw tears.

In the tiny little moment she saw it all, clearly away from Misra, detached from Surjit. Singular, alone, free, self-possessed moment. Challenging the lifeless past and the artificial future of this room.

Had she not stood in this dense darkness, she might never have seen clearly beyond this moment's core at the path etched before her. Missed its infectious courage!

She realised that now she would be able to break away – from Misra's physical oppression and Surjit's emotional violence self-contained; alone.

Something leapt inside her. Clear, alive; irrefutable. She arrived barefoot outside Dr. Agnihotri's clinic where she had once accompanied a colleague.

"I need help doctor!" Her eyes were cold and resolute.

The doctor looked her over and handed her the form.

"That won't be necessary. No one will share the responsibility for my abortion," she said calmly.

"You mean...?"

"I was raped."

A Girl Called Stella

P. Lankesh

Stella came, the nurse, olive-complexioned and with clean tapering fingers, cheeks with a touch of fading youth and thick hair. She was Subbanna's favourite. He thought no end of her. If only she could be on duty both day and night! He thought that her body exuded a smell of motherhood. He would know as soon as she entered the room. Once he had dared to ask her. Will you come and nurse me if I were to shift to my son's place? I'll pay you for it and make sure you don't lack anything. Stella had said nothing. She had patience and could be stern too. She had given him his pills and medicine and left without answering. Even her indifference, which he thought was divine, had whetted his curiosity about her. Not having enough courage to ask her again, he had started talking about himself. Subbanna hailed from a village near Shimoga. Having sold his property there, he had settled down in Nellandur near Bangalore and owned two houses besides a farm.

Stella had given her answer later. "It'll cost you Rs 300 a

day. Don't take me amiss. That's the fees which our association has fixed. I can't accept anything less than that."

Fear and pain. Subbanna started coughing. He knew he was going downhill, both morally and physically.

His son and daughter-in-law visited him, as usual, promptly at eight o'clock. The son looked wasted, Subbanna's illness had taken its toll. The daughter-in-law too looked run down. They used to stay with him in the hospital before. Subbanna himself had felt bad about it and was in two minds for a while before he had sent them home.

The doctor too came in just as Suresh and Savithri arrived. After having examined the patient and talking to Stella, he told Suresh that he would like to have a word with him.

"Something private?" Suresh asked the doctor.

"Nothing like that. You father's all right but we have to change the treatment. The drugs are expensive and there's need for surgery besides.

The dialysis will cost you at least Rs 200 a day."

"Why are you bringing up the matter of money?" asked Subbanna while Suresh sat with his head bent. The doctor explained, "It's better for us to be frank about matters. There should be no misunderstanding later. What do you say, Suresh?"

Suresh sat there saying nothing. He didn't either shake his head or look at his wife who seemed to be avoiding his eyes.

The doctor obviously had decided on surgery. "It'll cost

you nothing less than a lakh."

Subbanna had his eyes closed. Suresh and Savithri stayed silent and their silence had in it the explosive potentiality of lightning. Subbanna was beginning to grasp the truth. The doctor ended up saying, "Do think about it. I don't mind if you admit him into another hospital."

Suresh broke his silence. "Let't not worry about money, doctor. Do carry on with the treatment."

His voice was heavy. A nice young man, he was Subbanna's only son and worked as an English lecturer in a college. They had two children and Savithri was a smart woman with no touch of meanness in her. A graduate in Commerce, knowing typing and with a Senior's Certificate in music, she could have taken up a job, if she wanted. She hadn't, fully occupied as she was in looking after the farm and her children. There was no time to spare either for reading or listening to music.

Subbanna was aware of the turmoil in Suresh's mind even though the boy had reassured the doctor about footing the bill. He said, "Listen, boy. Let me die. What's there to live for, now that I'm eighty-five? A couple of years more shouldn't matter at this stage of my life. Why should you spend all that you have and get into a scrape?"

"It's not that, father. What's my own worth if I can't look after you when you are ill?" Savithri had placed her hand fondly on the old man's forehead, in support of her husband.

The truth was different, cruel. Subbanna was overwhelmed

by his fear of death. There was no ring of conviction about his question, 'What's there to live for?' Years ago, the thought of death brought no fear to him. It was different now – thinking of death brought tears to his eyes. Another cruel truth was that his illness had reduced his own son to a small-minded man. Deep down, beneath his words, there was the question why should not death come naturally to his father instead of bothering him in this manner. Suresh was crying inside of him as much as his father. His financial situation had become precarious. He had spent eight thousand on nursing his father in the first year, and later a lakh. He had borrowed from every available source and his debts were weighing him down. He had already sold the farm and it might even become necessary to sell the house they now lived in along with the one that Subbanna had rented out. It wouldn't matter – he still had his lecturer's job. Who knows, the fact that he was a debtor might affect his work. The farm that Savithri doted on was gone and her spirits were low though she had managed to hide the fact from others.

One day, Suresh was late in coming for a visit, The farm had gone by then and he was once again deep in debt. He was involved in a minor accident as he rode his scooter on his way to the hospital. He wasn't hurt but something had given way inside. Subbanna, who himself was in a foul mood, took one look at his son and said, "I know what you are thinking."

Suresh kept quiet.

"And you know what I'm thinking about you."

Suresh kept his silence and that infuriated his father more. Summoning whatever strength he had in him, Subbanna heaped abuses on his son, pounding his bed, Suresh said nothing. Subbanna started coughing blood. He desired to die at that moment of frenzied anger but was afraid. Stella arrived. Unperturbed by the spittle which trickled out with drops of blood, she cleaned him. Her brows were knit at Subbanna's behaviour. Subbanna lay back and as Suresh got up wanting to leave, his father tried to say something. Was it an attempt to make peace with his son or ask for forgiveness? Subbanna himself didn't know. He was seized by a fresh bout of coughing which wouldn't stop. Stella massaged his neck and his back. As Suresh slowly walked out, he heard his father shout, "Listen, bastard, I don't want either that bitch of yours or you here! Understand?" Suresh walked away, his head bent.

Alternating between fever and sleep, deep down, Subbanna feared that it might be the state of coma which normally precedes death. He was at that stage when sleep and unconsciousness shed their difference the way good and evil or shame and self-respect did. Stella didn't have enough energy in her to explain things to him. She was in charge of three patients in two wards and besides, she had her own personal problems. Her husband, Smith, had started drinking heavily. He was pressurising her to sell the three acres of wet land she had in Malabar and hand over the money to him. She had a feeling that he would leave her as soon as he laid his hands on the money. Their child, Nick, who spent the entire daytime in a nursery was never far from her thoughts, leading her to ask herself whether there was any point to her life.

"Amma ..." Subbanna groaned, its tone both an outlet for his pain and summons to Stella. He didn't mind if the girl didn't come in answer. His use of various endearing forms of address had increased as his helplessness grew. He hadn't left his bed for many days even for his excretory functions. His back was covered with bed sores and he wasn't aware that his legs had stiffened as they stretched from under the sheet that covered his body. He was either in a state of daze or coma though Stella was sure that his brain functioned normally as he was aware of his state.

Stella was there when he called out 'Amma .' Subbanna extended his hand and she asked him what he wanted. His eyes pleaded for her hand and she touched his hand with hers. He caught hold of her young and warm fingers and hand and cried out, "Child, my child." His eyes shone as if a new life coursed through him. The increasing warmth of his touch made it clear to Stella that it wasn't a father's hand caressing his child. "Will you do something for me, please?" he asked, She had been nervous whenever he came out with such a question. It was no different this time though she asked, "What?" A dirty old man. She told herself.

"Never mind," he said and let go of her hand. The fear in

his eyes was that of a man being led to the gallows. His lips started moving even as she watched.

"I haven't wiped my bottom myself for three years..." He started crying and Stella's stern heart melted. She held his hand which lay on his chest and his tear-filled eyes spoke of his gratitude. His other hand covered the back of her hand and he started muttering to himself. His words were about her, himself, the world, the gallows and death which could have been lurking just outside the room.

"I wasn't like this once, so miserable and so dirty... Do you believe it?"

Stella made no comment. She hadn't been able to check his bedsores. Subbanna seemed to have forgotten them of late.

"1950. I should have died that year."

"Eh, Stella ..." It was Mary.

Stella's eyes asked what it was about.

"Francis is here," Mary said.

"I see." As Stella slowly got up, a shiver passed through her. Francis, who had said he would try to meet her, had actually turned up.

She was, however, reluctant to leave Subbanna's side as if she was face to face with an unexpected truth. "Stay here, I'll be back in five minutes." Stella made Mary take her place, placed her friend's hand on Subbanna's. "Just five minutes," she repeated and left.

Francis was there. Stella's legs were giving way unable to carry her body, trembling from head to foot in sheer excitement.

"Is your husband back?"

Stella didn't reply, There was dense darkness to the left of the nursing home, under the thick foliage of the poppy, on the nearside of the shrub with white flowers.

She went into his arms and he kissed her, caressing her body with his hand. It was like kissing a flame – her longing was more intense than ever.

"It would be nice if you came today, I had thought," said Stella and he continued to kiss her.

"Let me go. Come tomorrow." Stella wriggled out of his embrace. Francis stood there, shocked, like a swimmer suddenly caught in a whirlpool. He didn't move till she had disappeared.

"All right?" Mary asked. There was still a mild tremor running through Stella's body and her face was flushed.

She took Mary's place and Subbanna opened his eyes wide as soon as he felt her hand, It was as if new vitality had come into him. "Will you carry out a dying man's wish, girl?" he asked. He didn't wait for her reply before he added, "It's my will. Take it down. It's a strange one. Please write it the way I want."

Stella took out a pen and a sheet of paper. Subbanna had difficulty in turning over before he lay on his stomach. His bed sores had started troubling him.

"I, who should have died in1950, am now certain that I shall die." He started sobbing and Stella read what she had taken down to stop him crying. "It was a grave mistake on my part to have avoided death at that time. My friend, Palakshappa died that year. He was a wrestler and I used to call him Palakshi. He was five years my senior and he would have been ninety, had he lived on. Nehru would have been a centurion, it seems, and Gandhi one hundred and twenty, had they been living... My grandfather, one hundred and fifty. I had vowed to offer a special service to Dharmasthala's Manjunatha if he were to die. Imagine his being alive at one hundred and fifty – a bag of bones, flesh and mucus...What could one do with such a living thing ...?"

"Come to the will, will you? Otherwise I'm leaving," Stella warned him.

"Why? The priest in our place was saying ... Take down ... It seems Bishma was a thousand when he died. What problems cropped up because the fellow forgot to die and went on and on..."

His cough brought him back to the world around.

"Palakshi was my friend, gentle like a cow, though an old wrestler. The men of the neighbouring village bothered him no end. Did I tell you that he was older than me by five years? Knowing that he would not retaliate, Goolya, Kaddipudi and Sannabasava of that village stole his crop of beans from the field. He went over to them and advised them to mend their ways. The same fellows later stole his sugarcane and then some bundles of hay. Palakshi didn't lose his temper. Encouraged by his attitude of tolerance, Goolya and Kaddipudi connived with the Shanbogh, forged some documents, called false witnesses and laid claim to two acres of his land. Palakshi asked for a meeting of the Panchayat saying that things shouldn't happen that way. Goolya and Kaddipudi saw to it that no one turned up for the meeting. I was upset and so went with Palakshi to meet the Shanbogh. Wasn't he a smooth talker, that bastard? He wriggled out of it and Palakshi kept quiet for three days as if he had been struck dumb. He didn't miss his daily trip to the smithy, though. Later he came to me with a question: Who was the most evil of them all and how would I arrange them in order of their evil. Early one morning, he sharpened his sickle and chopped them up, one after another. First, the Shanbogh and then Goolya, Kaddipudi and Sannabasava in that order. He returned to our village and so did the police. He died on the gallows six months later with a smile on his face.

"Mustn't forget it. I wasn't in the village when the police came. Though Palakshi didn't name anyone in that affair, it's true that I had my own apprehensions and so left the village. Palakshi would have been ninety if he were alive now. I still carry in me a vivid picture of his bearing – chest thrust forward. He had killed men and then gone to the gallows . Incidents of robbery, forgery, etc. declined in our village following the event.

Are you taking down what I'm saying? The reason why I told you all this is ... Isn't my will like a story, girl?" What started as a small cough grew and Subbanna's body shook.

"Our Abubakker Sahib used to drink. He had a proud bearing and looked like an Englishman. He was a contractor in Shimoga and had plenty of money. We were very close and used to frequent each other's houses. My wife, Parvathi, didn't like him, thought he was an evil man. Parvathi was a good woman, the daughter of the Patel of Ramenally. You don't know how good looking she was... like Parvathi in the picture of Shiva and his consort, like the actress Bhanumathi. One day I was in Abubakker's place playing cards with him and some others. We had drinks and were talking loudly. Suddenly, a minor quarrel erupted and Abubakker said something nasty. I was drunk and called him the son of a mean-minded beggar. When he said I had no balls, I wanted to leave the place but didn't. We carried on hurling abuses at each other. A drunken quarrel, it went on and on. 'I'll sleep with your wife, you wait,' he said and I shouted that I would do the same. We didn't come to blows, though."

"On Sunday, the fourth. It was the night of the fourth. There was a knock on the door and I sat there petrified. Parvathi opened the door to let in Abubakker who straightaway grabbed her. I was on fire and wanted to hit him but he tied me to a pillar in the living room, gagged us both and switched off the light. He had been drinking that night, I was sure.

"You may not believe it, but the unthinkable had happened. He had left but the lights weren't switched on. Parvathi sobbed the whole night. She had been humiliated and felt bad about what had taken place and so didn't look at me when it was morning again. I was burning with rage the whole day as Parvathi didn't bother to get up even once. When it was dawn again, I got up and looked for the sickle that Palakshi had used but couldn't find it. That evening I went to Budensabi's place, thrust some money into his hands and took his revolver. By the time I reached Shimoga, my anger had abated. I tried to whip up my thirst for vengeance and started walking round Abubakker's house. It was dark and there were the mosquitoes, droning away. I was furious with myself. When the rear door of the house opened, there was Abubakker turning the torch on me. He called out my name. Didn't laugh or say anything nasty. He took me by my hand and led me in. When I didn't respond to his smooth talk with either rage or laughter, he threw in the last dice. 'Forget it, pal. I'll give you one of my four farms...'

"The farm was registered in my name within four days.

"Parvathi didn't get up again. I don't know whether she came to know of my compromise or whether her shame was beyond all words. She died.

"That was in 1950. Abubakker died five or six years after the event. He would have been eighty-eight had he lived and would be lying on his sickbed just as I'm doing."

Stella stopped writing and got up. It was late, past her hours of duty.

"Do you know why I told you all this? Just a minute, girl. We go on saying that it's better to live like a tiger for a day than like a mouse for a hundred years. It's a cliché. Look at my lot, having to lie in my own piss and shit. My son has become evil but he behaves as if he's good, I too am evil but haven't got strength enough even to pretend to be good. I have often thought during the last ten years that I should have chopped off Abubakker's head and smeared Paravathi's forehead with his blood. I wouldn't have been the hypocrite that I am now. Or, I should have protested and died like the others in 1960 when the government raided our village to collect dues and attached our properties... This is the last sentence of my will, girl. It's not how long a man lives that makes his life. No, it certainly doesn't..."

"Lie down quietly," Stella said and left after placing what she had taken down under the cot. The nursing home was quiet. When she left after bidding the watchman goodnight, Francis was still there. She was feeling somewhat out of sorts and had been dreaming about how nice it would be if Francis were to be there and there he was. She ran to him and hugged him. "Let's walk till Benson Town," he suggested. It was cool and at ten in the night, Bangalore was quiet as usual. They were about to set off when they saw someone like Stella's husband coming towards them. "I think it's Smith," she said, a little nervous, and moved away from Francis. Yes, it was Smith. Stella and Francis pretended to be mere acquaintances as they approached him. Smith. talked to his wife pleasantly and she introduced Francis to him as a matter of course.

"Come, let's have a drink. It's a pleasure meeting you", said Smith. Stella watched both men closely as they struck up a friendship. Francis started talking about his bank and Smith gave an enthusiastic account of the garage he was about to open. Francis went on about the girl he was engaged to and addressed Stella as sister. "Sister, how's it that you haven't asked me home though you have such a wonderful husband like this? Look, it's settled. I invite myself with my fiancée to spend this year's Christmas at your place."

"Forgive me. I must go home. Nick will be waiting for me. Have a nice time together," Stella said.

"Why don't you also join us darling? I went home when I reached the city. You don't have to worry, I have taken care of everything. Let's talk about your land. It'll be so easy to open the garage if we were to sell it and take a small loan from Francis's bank."

Stella's head was reeling. "I've a headache, I better go home," Stella excused herself and the two men walked away.

Stella's head was filled with Subbanna's story. Subbanna, who could have died any time with a sense of either guilt or shame, now in living hell, a whimpering mouse because he couldn't live and die like a tiger. And her husband, who was ready for any kind of compromise or shame as long he could lay his hands on her land. And her lover, Francis, who was more complex and dangerous than even Abubakker. They were all dying, just like Subbanna after the year 1950. Dying even while living, caught in the mire of piss, shit and spittle and living in shame, scared of life and scared equally of death.

"Have a nice time," she muttered to herself. She sat in the rickshaw, sobbing with a strange sense of being utterly alone and utterly helpless.

"To Vaialikaval," she said in answer to the driver's enquiry and sobbed on.

That night, Subbanna died. There was a crowd by the time Stella turned up at the nursing home. Suresh and Savithri were by the bedside with tears in their eyes.

Stella couldn't look them in the eye. She went about silently helping to cart the body away.

The Saint and the Witch

Harkrishna Kaul

Tarachand died at five-thirty in the morning. The news reached Ramjoo's residence at seven. Immediately after, Ramjoo, Sonamal and Heebatani left Jawaharnagar for Bana Mohalla.

"Salutations to such a death!" said Ramjoo. "No pain, no illness. It was only the other day that I met him at Habbakadal. And we stood there a long time, talking of this and that. Do you know what he said to me that day? 'Let the weather hold a little, I'll come and spend a few days with you all at Jawaharnagar.' Ramjoo heaved a deep sigh and added, "only goes to show you – how near death is!"

"A fine release for him, nothing but snubs and knocks for the poor woman left behind", Sonamal said, "even the ones born from your own womb do not bother these days, what can you expect from an adopted son? Dear God, let me not live a day without my husband – let me go into your arms with all the marks of my marriage intact!", she wiped a tear with a corner of the long veil covering her head.

"Poor fellow, such a saintly soul he was! So obliging – always ready to help, be it friend or stranger. So good to everyone! And then he wielded such influence too – seemed to know everyone who mattered, and they held him in such high esteem", Ramjoo elaborated.

"He looked like Lord Indra himself", Sonamal gushed, "his parrot-green turban, almond-coloured *sherwani,* tight-fitting white trousers and feet shod in fine moccasins – how well they suited him! I have never seen his footwear unpolished."

"Well, he was certainly a 'gay cavalier' in his time," Ramjoo chuckled, "don't you remember the stylish angle his turban had? When Gasha was getting married, I – as the husband of his eldest aunt – was the one who had tied the bridegroom's turban. But the wretch had it untied and declared that he would not step out for the bride's place unless his turban was tied by Tarachand!"

"They say that even at this age he would walk up to Hari Parbat every morning," Sonamal touched upon another aspect.

"Not only that – he would spend every Saturday night at the feet of the goddess Chakreshwari; every *Ashtami* would find him before the Devi at Khir Bhavani."

"What a voice he had! One day I heard him singing *bhajans* at Khir Bhavani – it was just like so many bells ringing at once."

"He was a *RajYogi,* in fact. While seeming to enjoy all the luxuries of this life, he had attained a spiritual plane too high to be comprehended by us. Who knows what secret *mantras* he chanted?"

"That is exactly what stood by him at the end. They say that all great souls relinquish their bodies in this very manner : one minute they are there and the next, gone!"

"Didn't I say that one should salute such a manner of dying?"

Heebatani heard her brother and sister-in-law's comments in silence. Their words seemed to torment her. She wondered why they could not observe even a minute's silence. How could they be rushing off to Bana Mohalla with such enthusiasm? One would think they were going to a party. Did they not feel even a shred of sorrow at this sudden death – Tarachand's death? She herself was devastated, numbed with grief. Had she had even the least suspicion that Tarachand would be gone so soon, would she not have rushed to him, touched his feet and sought his forgiveness? Would she not have fallen at his feet and confessed that truly it was she – she alone – who was guilty of harbouring the sinful thought at that fateful time when she had almost destroyed the lifetime's achievements of a *Tapasvi*, a *rishi* like him. She was a sinner, she would have said, and asked for absolution from him. But alas, he had not even given her the opportunity for such penance; Tarachand's death had dealt her a blow the anguish of which would stay with her till death.

"There's no denying that Tarachand was a saint," Ramjoo

continued to eulogise the departed soul.

"A saint indeed ! A god, I would say," Sonamal corroborated heartily.

"Pure heart, pure eye and handsome like a god – that was Tarachand. And his wife? Ugly as sin. Yet he doted on her, ready even to hold out his palms to receive her spittle!"

"How right you are! A woman like Tarawati? What an absurd match for a man like him. The like of her does not deserve to be called a wife. No looks, no brains, no grace of any kind. Just a lump of flesh trailed by a veil."

"That may be so, but you can't deny that she is the real victim of this blow. Who can tell how Natha will treat her now, whether she will receive any comfort from him?"

"What comfort did *she* ever give him? As she has sown, so shall she reap."

"What can you expect from such a relationship? It is always the same in such cases : the mother never contented with the adopted child and the child equally disgruntled."

"How can you say that?" Sonamal countered, "Nathji is a real gem. And his wife Shanta, as meek as meek can be. The two of them would not allow Tarawati to lift a finger to do any work. More likely than not, it is your own offspring who is ready to pluck out your entrails these days." Sonamal tied the sash round her *pheran* a little more tightly.

"But Tarawati has raised Natha as her own from his infancy."

"As if I know nothing!" Sonanmal contradicted her husband, "I did not always live in a bungalow at Jawaharnagar (bless my Saiba for it!) Wasn't I their tenant for all those years? I know every bit of the goings on in that household. Not once have I seen her brow free from a frown – always a sour face, that one. Well, God also treated her the way she deserved. Better be a bitch than barren, that's what I think."

"How does it matter now? Our relationship was all with Tarachand – he is in heaven and the story ends."

"Yes, it was only he who knew how to maintain relations, the courtesies and graces of hospitality," Sonamal had still not exhausted herself talking. She continued, "As for *her* –the very sight of a guest would send her into mourning, as if her father had just died!"

Tarachand enjoyed life to the full, not only enjoyed all the luxuries himself, but ensured that others had them too. Actually he was in government service at a time when it meant something to be in it. Wherever he was posted, he received royal treatment. He did not have to suffer the indignities of this 'People's Raj too long either – he retired soon after it was imposed on us."

"Oh yes, he certainly did relish all the pleasures of this world. This must have been his only sorrow."

"To tell the truth, Tarawati is not so bad, only she is rather dumpy."

"I did not mean her looks alone – every woman cannot have the beauty of a *pari,* but this one seems to be a case apart.

Knowing full well that her husband was a man of refined taste, delicate feelings, a lover of cleanliness, tidiness and neatness, she should have paid some attention to her own grooming at least. But she seemed to find even washing her face a chore. Dressed in a rag of a *pheran,* there she would sit at a window, mourning God knows what. Her hair always tangled, the tresses lank with grime, she looked like a witch indeed – God save us from Evil!"

"But Tarachand never complained at all," Ramjoo said.

"Never!" Sonamal agreed, "he looked after her so well. You won't find such devotion even among the most modern of husbands."

"He was certainly a god incarnate, but his life was wasted and ruined by this witch."

Tarachand's life had been wasted and ruined – the realisation of this had dawned upon Heebatani before everyone else; perhaps because her own life had also been wasted and ruined. She has just completed fifteen years of age when she was married. Within five years she found herself a widow. But even out of those, more than three must have been spent in her parents' home.

All that was a thirty-year-old story. Today Heebatani could not even remember the face of the partner of that brief companionship. With the greatest effort, she could only stir a dim recollection of a vague form: an eighteen or nineteen-year-old Kashmiri Pandit youth, thinly built, shy. When she used to go up to the storeroom to bring down rice or spices, he would follow, stalking her. But the loud shout of, "Damodaraah!", from his mother's powerful lungs would send him scurrying like a dog with docked ears into the small room next door. How stern, how formidable his mother was! Far from giving the couple the privacy of a room of their own, she did not even allow them to exchange a few words with each other. The moment Heebatani returned from a long visit to her parents' house, her husband would find himself despatched to his maternal grandparents' place – so apprehensive was the mother of losing her grip on her son. But in spite of all her efforts, lose him she did in the very fifth year of his marriage, for ever. The mother herself did not survive the son more than a year. For a long time after, Heebatani could see nothing but desolation wherever she turned.

After her mother-in-law's death, her brother brought her home. For about a year she was looked after very well, but soon her sister-in-law put her to work, scrubbing and washing in the kitchen. Heebatani thought that this was what she had been made for. Accepting the finality of her fate, she plunged wholeheartedly into the drudgery and chores of her brother's household. Soon after, Ramjoo's relations with his collaterals soured, and as a result of the family dispute, he moved out and became a tenant in a portion of Tarachand's house. You could say, without fear of any contradiction that it was here that a new life was breathed into Heebatani, thanks to

Tarachand. He gave up going out in the evening after returning from work, taking up the task of imparting religious education to Heebatani instead. He would read out the *Ramayana, Mahabharata, Bhagwat* and *Shiva Purana* to her. He bought her copies of the *Bhagwadgita* and *Hanuman Chalisa* to study.

Instead of sweeping and mopping the floors in the mornings, Heebatani now went to the temple, Gently pouring water on a Shiva Linga. She also began to follow Tarachand's practice of observing the *Ashtami, Amavas* and *Purnima** as days of fasting and prayer. On these holy days, she would cook the ritual food – rice and vegetables – for Tarachand herself, simmering the sweetened milk till thickened, frying *pakoras* and potato chips and making *halwa* and sago *kheer* according to strictly laid down religious prescription. After he had been served and fed, she too would eat the same food. Tarawati could not have been too happy with Heebatani taking over these duties from her, but she could not say anything.

Heebatani went on pilgrimages to several holy places with Tarachand. On a number of *Ashtamis,* she went to Khir Bhavani with him. It was Tarachand who was responsible for her going to Bhavan in Mattan where at long last, she had the *shraddha* of the poor dead Damodar performed. Once when news came that a *sadhu* of great spiritual power had taken up residence in Chandigam, Tarachand took her along to seek his blessings. They stayed at the Sadhu Babaji's *ashram* for a night. The next afternoon they left for Sogam on their way home.

The memory of that fateful day sent shivers down Heebatani's spine even now. On the way, it had started raining – a sudden deluge that seemed to crush stones into sand with its fierce power. Drenched to the bone, their clothes dripped wet as though they had both had a dunking in the river. And to top it all, there was no bus for the town of Sogam. Fortunately Tarachand found an acquaintance in the overseer of the area. The overseer himself was away in Srinagar, but Tarachand had the *chowkidar* open his official residence for them. The *chowkidar* lit the iron stove and hugging its warmth, they dried their wet clothes. At about five, Tarachand went out and bought some meat and asked the *chowkidar* for some rice, oil and spices. Heebatani went into the kitchen and cooked a meal. After they had eaten, she spread the overseer's bedding for Tarachand. For herself, she took a couple of blankets and lay down. But sleep eluded her. There was not a moment's lull in the rain. The month of July had become as bitingly cold as December. She tossed and turned on the cold floor for a long time, unable to find rest. And then she quietly slipped under Tarachand's quilt. As her arm fell across his back, he woke up. Finding Heebatani in his bed, he leapt out, went to the pitcher of water, washed his hands and feet and sat down in the classic *asana* for meditation. Heebatani ran into the kitchen. In that refuge, she dug her teeth into her flesh. How she wished that the earth would open up and she jump into the abyss and disappear for ever. Her eyes turned into crumpled, dried apricots with incessant weeping. For a long time afterwards she could not meet Tarachand's eye. It was God's grace that soon after, they shifted to Jawaharnagar permanently. As they were leaving, there was a bitter altercation with Tarawati for some trifling reason, with the result that interaction between the two families ceased for the next few years.

A long time had passed since then. Heebatani was almost fifty now. Often the thought had occurred to her that she should go to Tarachand and seek his forgiveness for her sin. But perhaps the shame was too deep for her to face him – something always prevented her from carrying the thought out.

The road from Jawaharnagar to Bana Mohalla seemed too long even now. She was in mortal fear that they might have taken him away before their arrival.

It was eight by the time they reached Bana Mohalla. Tarachand's body was still there. A flower-bedecked plank had been prepared, and it lay waiting in the yard. There was a large gathering of people sitting on mats around, everyone of them relating the good deeds of the departed. Ramjoo sat down among them, Sonamal and Heebatani went in. Seeing them, Tarawati and a few other women set up a loud wail. Sonamal went close to Tarawati and pressing a handkerchief to her lips, stopped her from crying. Heebatani did not go near Tarawati. She went up to where Tarachand had been laid on a bed of grass. Taking hold of the dead man's feet, she wept profusely, emitting loud cries of, "Oh my father, brother, Guru!"

After a while she rose, prostrated herself before Tarachand's body and said, under her breath, 'It is true that I was the one enfolded by darkness. Please forgive me my sin. This life of mine was a complete waste and ruin, let not the same happen to my next one. I must have your forgiveness.'

Tarachand's body, laid on the plank, was carried away at about eleven, elaborately decorated with wreaths and garlands of fresh flowers. Just before the pall-bearers lifted the plank, an expensive shawl was spread on it. Tarawati followed the funeral procession into the alley, weeping and wailing loudly. She was brought back, a couple of women supporting her. Once inside, she sat quietly for a long time stunned in silence. Then, all of a sudden, she burst out to the women gathered before her, "Forgive me, sisters – for fifty years the seal on my lips has not been broken, but now that he has left the house, I must speak. Look at me, even now I am that seven-year-old, untouched, unravished child bride!"

Heebatani seemed to fall from a great height. It was as though a light had begun to shine upon several dark corners an answer given to many an old puzzle. She rose and took the other woman in her arms, and the two women howled together.

Sumati

Hemacharya

Only when the nurse came to me and called 'Grandma'. I returned from my imaginary world. I had lost control of myself and was sitting there.

"Grandpa, tears in your eyes ...!"

Unknown to me my hand went to my eyes. Yes, my eyes were filled with tears. Looking at the pretty, fair face of the nurse, I tried to smile. But no smile would come.

"What were you thinking. Grandpa? About your family ...?"

"No, my child," I said with affection. "When I have you, such a darling grandchild, with me, why should I think of my family?" I patted her back.

"Grandpa, don't worry, your grandchild brought an injection for you." Laughing, she pricked my left buttock with the injection, and, with her sparkling laughter, walked away. Once again I was lonely in my room.

There was just a week to Christmas. At the word 'Christmas' my thoughts flew back. My hair stood on edge.

My eyes were wet once again.

That particular day, sitting on my bed, I was eating the bread I was given, dunking it in the tea. The evening shadows had reached my room. Just then an innocent little girl passing by my side saw me, an old man on an old man's bed, and came near me. Seeing her I just smiled. Something in my eyes must have attracted her.

"Good evening ..." she said smiling.

"Good evening, Baby, what caste are you?" I asked her in Kannada.

"I am a Christian. Grandpa," she answered in Konkani. "My name is Sumati."

"Oh, I – I see!" As I was stuttering in my confusion, she began to ask: "Grandpa, what is wrong with you? Fever, cough ...?"

"No, my child, mine is not a big illness. Mine is a small illness – that of old age". I answered her with a smile.

'Oh', she said taking pity on me. I raised my head slowly and watched her. A tender, pretty face; ten years at most: a smiling face.

"I'll pray for you, Grandpa, Jesus will soon cure you ...", she said holding my hand.

"This is not the type of illness that can be cured, my child ..."

"All right ...", she said not knowing what to say. "Grandpa, shall I go now? We were told to return early after visiting the sick. But instead of coming here, all those girls are watching the game of cricket on the playground."

"Oh ..." I said, raising my hand to bless Sumati. "Go, my dear. Speaking to me you have lessened my pain. May God make you a good child."

"I will come to see you tomorrow evening too. Grandpa." Saying this, she jumped up like a gazelle and ran away like a butterfly. And I stayed there watching her pretty, peacock-like gait.

"What a loving child!" I thought to myself. "Out of a hundred God certainly creates an angelic girl." Then I was busy with my evening prayers.

Next evening I myself was waiting to see Sumati. She came before dark. Spoke kind words just as she did the day before.

"Grandpa, you look sad, don't you? What is your illness, Grandpa?"

I remained silent. Why should I ralse a tempest in the mind of such a small child telling her about my illness, I thought. But she did not let me go at that. Catching hold of my hand, she said: "Grandpa, don't you want to tell me? I will not tell anyone, Grandpa ..."

Then she herself must have felt that it was not right to worry the grownups. She changed the topic: "Grandpa, last night we had our prayers in common. I prayed that you might be cured soon. You will soon get well, Grandpa, and as soon as you get well, I will take you to the convent holding your hand."

I raised my head with a start, and glanced at her face: To the convent? I had not even suspected that such a pretty, innocent angel of a child was an orphan and was staying in the convent orphanage. Filled with pity, I kept looking at her face. Shyly, Sumati lowered her head and said: "Grandpa, why do you look at me like that?"

"Where do you stay, my dear? Your parents ...?"

"No Grandpa, I am unlucky. I have no parents nor anyone. I am an orphan, Grandpa, I stay in the convent." Her voice had weakened and her eyes were filled with tears.

With difficulty I got down from my bed and hugging her, I cried, "You are not an orphan, my dear; from today you are my grandchild – and I your Grandpa ..."

Sumati's eyes too were filled with tears of happiness mixed with tears of sadness, which shone like pearls before they ran down.

From then on Sumati came every evening. She would describe the qualities of her companions at the convent, and relate how they teased each other, and would please me with such other talk. After Sumati started coming to me, I felt that my suffering was abating. As evening approached, I would look forward to her visit, and once she went back, I would feel lonely and desperate as if missing something, and would start my evening prayers.

One evening Sumati did not come. All sorts of doubts began to bother me – "What has happened to the girl: Is she not well? Or did anything happen to her on her way to see me?" Many thoughts of this kind gave me a fright. My eyes were constantly turned to the door waiting for Sumati to come. But Sumati did not come. In desperation, I began to pray.

The next evening too she did not come. I could not wait any longer. With the help of my cane I went to the entrance of the hospital and sat on a wicker chair, and kept looking with my eyes fixed to the edge of the road in the distance. Sitting there I began to pray: "O God, protect my grandchild from every trouble, do not make me an orphan ..." Just then Sumati came there bringing a nun along with her.

She was the Superior of the Convent. She narrated to me the details of poor Sumati's life: Sumati was the daughter of an unwed mother. At dawn one day her mother abandoned her nine-month-old baby on the Convent steps. From that day all the nuns in the Convent took care of the helpless child in their orphanage, feeding her and raising her as their own little sister.

The sisters in the Convent treated her with affection. But Sumati's bad luck did not stop at her birth: for the last three years she suffered from severe bouts of asthma. By day she would play with her mates, go to school, but once it was night her suffering would begin. She would cough away lying on her stomach. The sisters did not leave her in the orphanage with the other children, but they would get her to sleep in the Convent itself. When her bouts of asthma were severe, some sister would take the child on her lap.

As the Superior of the Convent narrated Sumati's story, I was on the verge of tears. But I thought it was not right for me, a man, to cry in her presence, and I controlled my tears. When Mother Superior told me that asthma was the reason why the girl had not come the previous day, I felt great pity for her – wondered why I had not gone to see her even if it be with the help of my cane.

Picking up Sumati's medicine they returned. Before going, Sumati said with a sad voice: "Pray for me, Grandpa: I pray for you. Both of us are patients ..." and she went away smiling. But I could not smile.

From childhood I have been very fond of children. I could not bear to see a child suffer from any sickness. My own son suffered from asthma for several years and that asthma had sucked up his life too.

I had only one son. Close on him my young wife too died.

Thus at a very young age I too had become an orphan. Before this my parents had left this world. I did not have any near or dear ones. Because of my illness and in my old age there was no one to look after me, I had sought permanent shelter in this hospital some 40 miles from my village. I had offered all my properties to this hospital. Thus I have been taken care of in this hospital for the last fifteen years.

From one point of view this had become my home. The doctors and nurses were my family, but I don't know why I experienced severe loneliness. As I began to feel that there was no one of mine own in this world to understand my sufferings and to console me, I felt that my illness was getting worse. I was experiencing the loneliness of an ant moving about in a three-acre plot all by itself.

But when I heard Sumati's story, I felt that my orphaned state and illness was nothing at all.

How could I compare that orphan child's permanently orphaned state with my temporary loneliness after enjoying the joys of family life?

On subsequent days her asthma must have subsided a little. She would come every evening to see me. As I spoke to her, I would forget my old age.

One evening as Sumati came along there were wrinkles on her forehead, of fear, surprise, and wonder. I questioned her as if something special had taken place: "Sumati, why do you look so strange today?"

Equally eagerly, she asked: "Grandpa, why did you send money to the sisters? You do not have money for your own expenses. You do not go to work, do you. Grandpa ...?"

I laughed. The day before I had sent a cheque for Rs 2000 to the Superior of the Convent as my gift to meet Sumati's expenses. The nun must have told the girl about it. Quietly my aged hands began to play with Sumati's hair, and I told her: "I don't need money, my dear. What I lack is good health and a happy family life. But you have provided me that pleasure, my child. Isn't it the duty of the grandfather to help his grandchild? If it isn't so what sort of Grandpa would I be to you?"

My words must have convinced Sumati. She kept quiet and then thinking of something, said: "Grandpa, only ten more days to Christmas. They are making a large Christmas crib outside our chapel."

"Is that so? Bravo!"

"Shall I prepare a crib here in your room?"

I looked at her face. There was eagerness and joy on Sumati's face. In my hospital life, I had not seen a Christmas crib for fifteen years. I told her with pleasure: "Certainly, make a crib here, my child, I will be very pleased."

"On the feast day, Grandpa, shall we both go to mass together? I will ask Mother beforehand, I will hold your hand and take you to our chapel for Mass, shall I?"

With a heart filled with joy, I said, "Yes, my dear ..."

"Today I'll go back a little early, Grandpa, Christmas novena has started. I will pray for you: Good night, Grandpa."

The next day Sumati came in running and said: "Grandpa, yesterday I forgot to ask you one thing. When I was praying for you at the novena, Sister asked, "What illness is your grandpa suffering from?" Wouldn't it be better to mention your illness to God? Grandpa, what is your illness?"

I remained silent. I was not willing to cause any worry to such a tender child by telling her what I was suffering from. So I told her: "My illness is one of old age, my dear. Tell sister that it is the illness of an old man, my child. She will understand."

"In that case, does every old person have an illness, Grandpa?"

"Yes, my dear", I said, "but everyone's illness will not make it necessary to come to a hospital."

Before going back, she held my chin and said: "Grandpa, I know – you are hiding your illness from me – aren't you?"

The feast was approaching. The crib in my room was getting ready. Every evening Sumati would get busy with the Christmas crib without talking too much. She had brought a few statues from the Convent. If I felt like, I too would get down from my bed and help Sumati to make the crib.

Two days before Christmas the crib was ready. That day I told Sumati who had brought the statue of Baby Jesus to place in the crib: "Sumati, that statue should not be kept there today, but five minutes before the birth of Jesus."

"That's all right, Grandpa. Day after tomorrow I will get ready at night and come straight here first. Then let both of us go to Mass. Coming back from Mass let us place Baby Jesus in the crib, shall we?"

"All right, my dear", I said.

The next day Sumati brought some of the Christmas sweets prepared at the Convent to let me taste them. Both of us sat down together and ate the sweets. Sumati said: "Look Grandpa, all these days I obeyed you. But today you have to obey me, Grandpa."

"Yes …?" I looked at her anxiously.

"Before going to Christmas Mass, you have to tell me what your illness is."

"Yes, certainly I'll tell you tomorrow, my dear …"

There were no bounds to her happiness. She hugged me tight and said: "Grandpa, how good you are!" Then wishing me good night, she went back.

Christmas day had dawned. From morning I was bent low in front of the crib and prayed that Sumati might be rid of her asthma. Sumati had told me that she would not come that evening. She would come at night before going to Mass. I brought out my wedding suit from my box. It was many years ago that I went to Christmas Mass wearing this suit …!

I had to go to Mass at twelve that night. Wanting to get some sleep before that, I went to bed at seven itself.

I woke up only when someone called out. It was eleven o'clock in the watch in front of me. Sumati had told me that she would come at eleven. When I opened my eyes, a girl was standing in front of me. Just then she said: "Grandpa, Sumati will not be able to come to Mass, it seems. Her asthma is bad today."

I felt as if my head was hit by a stone. I sat up. The girl's lips were quaking.

"Where is she?" I asked desperately.

"She is in the Convent, Grandpa: she has sent me to go along with you to Mass."

"No, my dear, not for Mass; take me to the Convent. I want to see Sumati." I got ready to go.

"Don't worry, Grandpa, her asthma is not so severe today. It does not matter if you don't come. She will herself come here in the morning."

I was not quite satisfied. But hearing the girl's words, I was comforted a little. I sent the girl back and I went near the Christmas crib. Baby Jesus was not yet placed in the manger. I bent myself in front of the crib and began to pray: "Baby Jesus, you are to be born today. Cure my Sumati of her asthma. Give her strength to bear her suffering ..."

I myself don't know how long I spent praying that way. When I opened my eyes it was morning. I had bent over to pray and I had fallen asleep there.

I raised my head and turned my eyes to the crib. Baby Jesus was not yet placed there. When Sumati came we would place the statue there and greet each other, I decided.

Just then the Superior of the Convent came and stood there! Smiling, she took my hands in hers. "Happy Christmas, Grandpa ..." she said. I too greeted her. But my eyes were searching for Sumati.

"Where is Sumati, Mother?" I asked her unable to suppress my impatience.

Her eyes were filled with tears. Rubbing her hands in a quaking voice she said: "Grandpa, Jesus has called your grandchild to his embrace ..."

As if thunderstruck, holding my hands to my ears I sat down bent over on my bed. Mother Superior went on: "Yesterday her asthma was not too bad. She even got herself ready to come here. But, but ..."

I began crying like a child abandoned by a mother. "Though I have been suffering for three years from cancer, God has left me behind and taken my tender grandchild, hasn't He, Mother ...?" My eyes were shedding tears uncontrollably.

"Take courage, Grandpa," said Mother Superior, "From heaven she will obtain salvation for you ... Even with her last breath she was calling out: Grandpa, Grandpa ..."

I was silent now. After consoling me for an hour and a half, Mother Superior turned back with heavy steps. But I was in no need of any consolation from any one. Slowly I turned my gaze to the crib. Baby Jesus was not yet placed there.

Going in I brought the statue of Baby Jesus. As I placed it between Joseph and Mary my eyes filled up with tears again. I prayed silently: "Jesus Christ, my Sumati worked hard to prepare a place for you to be born in this world. But you did not allow both of us to experience the joy of your birth. Grant her eternal rest ..."

Among the thousand people who gathered in the evening for Sumati's funeral, I was the closest to her.

"Grandpa, why are you crying? I have news of joy for you. The doctor says that your blood has cleared. You have been saved from the terror of cancer ...!" When I looked at the nurse, she gave me a broad smile.

"All this is due to Sumati's prayer, sister!" I gratefully remembered my grandchild.

"Oh, you have been thinking about Sumati! Don't cry Grandpa, can't I become your grandchild in place of Sumati?"

Once again I glanced at the nurse's face. At the same time I began to think: "Who would be able to give me such a pure love as the one that Sumati did?"

Didn't I Know It!

Manipadama

Unusually bright eyes. Like those of a startled doe. As though woken out of a nightmare. In a dazzling white saree of homespun khadi. Around sixteen years of age. Gold-brown complexion. Full of energy, ready to help everybody. Unassuming.

At the Khadi Bhandar, it is the week-day for the local spinners. Among the elderly women gathered there, she looks like a lone lotus blooming in the middle of a reed-filled little pond. She would enjoy the day fighting the Khadi Bhandar workers on behalf of the women-spinners, who have brought their piles of thread.

The workers would smile at her. They would weigh the piles of thread again reassign numbers[1] to them, count out the money and hand it to her. She would then tell each of them how much their thread had been valued at and distribute the cash. She would number the very coarse ones “”hundred-and-fifty” and the really fine ones “ten” Sometimes it took a long time, the worker in charge would get annoyed and chide her.

She would lose interest then and turn aside to sit by herself in a corner and the elderly manager's eyes would fill with tears; he would remark soothingly, with affection. "Sanjha *dai,*[2] Khadi Bhandar is not a commercial set-up : it's our own organisation, you know, Do please help the workers and the spinners, don't take offence like this." And once again Sanjha would return, and her haggling on the spinners' behalf would be merrily resumed.

And yet when her own turn came, Sanjha would not say a word. Her own pile was the biggest and her thread the finest but she would smile sadly and say, "*Bhaiji,*[3] I won't say anything about my own work. Give it the number you like." That day the Bhandar was very crowded. She was helping everyone as usual. The one thing beyond doubt was that the worker in charge of buying tht piles of thread relied a lot on her numbering of the piles.

"Number fifteen to this angry old woman's thread," she would say as she pushed the pile forward. "Thirty bundles. May be it could be finer, may be she had an argument with her daughter-in-law before she started spinning!"

"Number forty to my big sister-in-law here!," she would announce, with the work of a complete stranger in her hand. "Big brother's been living away from the village a long time ; so my sister, takes a lot of interest to pass the time at the spinning wheel."

And the woman referred to as sister-in-law looks up and

her face suddenly lights up, she says, "O dear, you do seem to know all about everyone!"

The ripples of laughter spread all around the circle of spinners. Then an old woman enters it from one side, a pile of thread in one hand, as though she is on fire. She seems to be mightily jealous of the sixteen-year-old.

"What are you doing here?" she says, angrily chiding her.

"What 'ginger-and-cotton'[4] of yours have I caused to be grazed on, that you come on me like a cobra with its hood spread?"

Sanjha is smiling at the old woman as she says this. The cobra hisses at the worker in charge, "Please weigh her pile of thread quickly, the poor unfortunate fool of a girl!"

Everyone is stunned and the cobra cannot help breaking the news, "Her family in the village is going through an emergency. Bad news from her in-laws' place. Her husband is no more!"

And everyone is expecting to see Sanjha going down like a creeper on a worm-eaten tree in the storm, but her face stays serene. Just as a flame reflected in a mirror does not in the least affect the peace, the patience and the glow of the mirror itself.

"So why do you come at me like a thunderbolt, old woman?"

She says simply, "I've known this since the night I was married."

A sixty-five-year-old skeleton of an ailing man and a twelve-year-old ... how long could it last? Didn't I know it. Oh, only too well, Come on, let me get your pile weighed too.'

Then she pauses a little.

"Oh, what to do about these coloured things," she says and starts breaking the glass bangles on both her hands at a spinning-wheel that she happens to be sitting near, Then she wipes off the red mark in the parting of her hair with her pile of thread, smiling and remarking to the worker in charge, "You'd never have numbered your thread with such a number, with your colour! Go on, weigh the piles. Whatever's happened that work should be interrupted? Shouldn't people live in this world? Shouldn't they die?"

And then she tried to smile again.

Let's Ask the Psychologist

Paul Zacharia

Respected Doctor,

Let me introduce myself. My name is Asha Matthew. Age 26. House-name, Karippurath. Father's name, Joseph Matthew. Address: Kattirampu P.O. Kuttiyadi. I am a young woman with a post graduate degree in English Literature and a B.Ed. degree. I have parents, an elder brother and two younger sisters. My brother is married. He has bought some land in Mananthavady and has settled down there. My sister-in-law is a teacher in a school there. One of my younger sisters is in the first year of the M.B.B.S. course. The youngest one is in the first year of the pre-degree course.

My father's father is a farmer who migrated to Kuttiyadi from Marangattupalli to escape famine conditions during the time of the Second World War. I have always argued with Grandfather, maintaining that he should not have cut down the forest and cultivated the land. But Grandfather's answer would be this: 'Asha, you have never had to starve. When one has starved for some days along with one's wife and children, one would feel like clearing, let alone forests, but the world itself and growing food.

Grandfather, aged 89, is a rationalist. He had carried on a correspondence with Dr. A.T. Kovoor, the renowned rationalist from Ceylon. In the evening when the family gathered for prayers, he would sit in his room and read. It was Grandmother, now 82, who made my father and all the rest of us follow in God's path. Every morning Grandmother would go to church walking the four kilometres. When Father bought a car and said he would drop Grandmother at the church, she said, standing in the yard with the church-going veil drawn over her hair, "I will go to the Lord's presence only on these two legs of mine, as long as I am able to walk." When I heard that I remembered the song in a Raj Kapoor film,

Sajan re jhoot mat bolo...

O upright ones, do not tell lies

You must go to God

Not on an elephant's back, nor on horseback

But only on foot.

When I burst out laughing thinking of this, Grandmother was incensed. 'Hey you, Asha, why are you laughing?" she asked.

My father is a member of the Congress party and a believer who lives according to the tenets of the Catholic Church. He conforms to all norms of gentlemanly conduct. Father had starved when he was very young. By the time he had reached the age when his stomach would digest even stone, Grandfather had already raised tapioca and paddy in Kuttiyadi. He has bagged the prize for model farmer many times. Father's love for us is beyond words. For him, our mother is precious. Father would drive Mother to bashfulness every now and then mentioning the fact that it was he who acted as midwife when she delivered our brother, because there was no doctor or hospital for miles around and Grandmother was away in the church. Father would ring up both my younger sisters in their hostels once a week regularly. Once a month he would visit them with a mountain of gifts. When I was in the hostel also, Father would do the same thing. If he couldn't get the books I had a fancy for in Kerala, he would order them from bookshops in Delhi. That's how I read Ethan Canin, Raymond Carver and Castaneda.

Though I have read them all, I am still a very simple person, doctor. I am neither an intellectual nor a revolutionary. From general observation, I have come to the conclusion that the opinion held by the people of the locality, my family members, my teachers and even my friends about me is that, I am a good-looking and well-behaved young woman. I can firmly state that till now no one ever had an occasion to complain about me.

I have lived a disciplined life, obedient to my parents, respecting my teachers and elders, loving my family and friends, and in submission to the teachings of the Church. I haven't been infatuated even with Mohanlal (renowned film star), whom I like most of all. My only wish is that I should be able to live the rest of my life quietly with a husband as gentle as my father and be a model wife, like my mother. It was not to earn a living that I studied English Literature and did the B.Ed. course. It was just to spend time till my marriage, learning, studying and reading what I liked and to enjoy the company of friends. I guess my father knew what was in my mind, although I had never told him explicitly.

Doctor, my mother is a pure-hearted, compassionate and loving woman. By the time Father married Mother, our family had become quite affluent. Mother came from a family in Mukkom that was still in financial straits. Grandfather had made all his three sons marry without demanding a dowry. Some time during his frequent *padayatras* of the Seva Dal and fund-raising peregrinations, Father had seen Mother and was captivated by her beauty. He then enquired about her and went ahead with a proposal. Grandmother herself said she had opposed it then. She said, 'Asha, there is something ominous about a woman who is exceedingly beautiful. However, your mother, though very good-looking, is a good woman.' My mother is a good, loving and innocent person free of all anxiety. When Mother had come as a new bride, Grandfather had tried to convert her into rationalism. Listening attentively to everything he said, she finally spoke, bashfully: 'Father, would you be angry with me if I refuse to believe that there is no

God?' Grandfather answered in the negative, saying, 'I believe that there is God." She ran off. Grandmother had then said, 'So long as there are such women in this family, God wouldn't be deprived of anything.' It's Mother who told me all this. I have always wanted to live like Mother until my death. I never had any loftier ambitions.

Doctor, I who lived in peace in such a loving family, am now facing a crisis. Two months ago, Mother asked me, "Asha, are you planning to study further?" 'No, Mother,' I replied. Then Mother put her arms around my shoulders, drew me to her side and asked,' 'Shall we look for a match for you, then?' Abashed, I leaned my head on her breast and agreed That night, I lay in bed for a very long time unable to sleep, looking out of the window at the fireflies glowing among the peppervines. After some time, the moon rose. When the moonbeams fell on my bed, I felt thrills running all over my body. Then I slept.

The first proposal came from a college lecturer. In the Tata Sumo he himself drove were his father, mother, sister and brother-in-law. As I finished handing out coffee and snacks to everyone, he asked me, lighting a cigarette: 'Didn't you try for jobs, after doing your B.Ed?' 'No,' I said. 'She doesn't want to take a job,' Father said. I felt that his lighting the cigarette was a cruel joke he unleashed unwittingly. He who sat there blowing out smoke, was handsome and very manly. When they left, I turned the fan on to full speed. Grandfather said, 'It is so cool.

Switch off the fan, my dear.' 'It's not that,' said. I didn't like him asking me questions, while lighting a cigarette.' No one said anything more about that. Grandfather said as if addressing everyone present, 'More grooms will come. Never mind.'

When I lay down that night, I began thinking; I know him as far as that cigarette and the Tata Sumo. Beyond that, everything about him is what I don't know. Suppose I had liked the lighting of the cigarette. How would I have ever learned the things I needed to know? Mother covered me with a sheet, made the Sign of the Cross on my forehead and intoned, 'Jesus!'

I liked the one who came to see me next. There was good-heartedness and softness writ on his face. He was a bank officer. After coffee and snacks, he said with a smile, "I too had studied English Literature.' Then we parted ways. After the group had left, everyone at home looked at me. I stood smiling, my head bent. That night I thought: I know him as far as English Literature. And I imagine his softness and good-heartedness. What would there be beyond that? Are there books in his house? Or just the old English Literature textbooks? Can I sleep there with the windows open? Would they season the chutney for dosa with sliced onion and mustard fried in oil? I like it that way. I tossed and turned for quite some time that night before I slept. The next day the marriage-broker came with the news that they liked me. However, the groom was active in the charismatic renewal movement of the Church. He is troubled that the girl's grandfather is a rationalist. 'No.

Let it go,' Father said looking at me. Grandfather glanced at me with a sense of guilt. I whispered in his ear, 'Don't bother, Grandfather! Grooms will come yet again.'

My marriage was fixed with the third boy who saw me. Their house was at Kozhikode. They had migrated from Ettumanur to Mukkom, and bought land near my mother's house and engaged in agriculture. They had built a house in the city in which they were living. The groom was an architect. It was fair-mindedness and friendliness that I saw on his face. 'Are you interested in taking a job?' he asked me. 'No,' I said. 'I too like it that way,' he said. 'I am managing business and agriculture together. But I like agriculture better.'

Doctor, my dilemma begins from here. On the night I got to know that the marriage was fixed, I lay in my bed looking out of the window with a sense of my life having reached a crossroads. It was dark outside. When a chilly breeze swept in through the open window, I covered myself from head to foot. Next when I awoke, there wasn't light even in Grandfather's room, where he would usually be reading well past midnight. The house was totally asleep. There was starlight outside. Suddenly, with a start, I thought: I... I am going away, leaving this house behind. I am going to another house, leaving behind Father, Mother, Grandfather, Grandmother, my younger sisters, this bed, this window, the kitchen, the well, the cowshed, and the helpers and labourers. I will stay in the other house, till my death. I will live among the people in that house.

Architect Joy's fair-mindedness and friendliness. What is there beyond these? As for Joy, he has seen my house. Saw the way to this house. Saw these hills and farmlands. Saw Grandfather and the books, Saw our dog Tatu. Saw the framed family photos hung up on the wall.. Saw the pepper that was spread out on a reed mat in the yard to dry. Saw the cows in the cowshed. Of course Joy did not know that it was while sitting on that settee on which he was sitting that I first menstruated. What about me? Like my Granddfather who migrated once and for all from Marangattupalli to Kuttiadi, I too shall migrate from my house for ever to Joy's house. What do I know about them? What all are there ? Do they love cows and goats? Do they cherish womenfolk, and show them loyalty? Do they eat the njalippoovan variety of plantains? Do they treat their servants with affection? Do they beat children making them scream? Do they chase away dogs and kick cats? Do they tease beggars? Do they wear clean underclothes? Do they tell lies and covet others' wealth? Do they respect books? Do they keep alive jealousy and hatred in their minds even while praying? Do they keep their doors and windows open? What are the crops on their farms? What time do they go to sleep? What time do they wake up? Do they have clean toilets? Do they drink their water boiled? Do they make their curry adding coccum? Do they cook their rice well?

Doctor, I felt as if I was falling through the darkness into a bottomless pit. Screaming inside me, I struggled up and sat bolt upright on the bed. For the first time I felt that I was all alone in this world. Shivering in the cold, I touched my hair, breasts and abdomen. A young woman called Asha Matthew. 26 years old. M.A.B.Ed. Daughter of Karippurath Joseph Matthew.Virgin. Have read T.S.Eliot and Hemingway. I touched my lips and eyes. Ran my fingers over my legs. Again I felt as if I was skidding through darkness and losing my grip. Don't scream, Asha Matthew, I told myself. When I got over that feeling, I lay down in the bed quaking to my bones and covered myself from head to foot.

I got up late. 'My dear daughter's face looks awful,' my mother joked. 'Have you begun to feel scared thinking about marriage?' I smiled and said nothing. After breakfast, I went to Grandfather's room and said in a whisper. 'Grandfather, I have a secret to tell you.' Taking off his reading glasses, he placed a bookmark where he left off reading, and motioned me to sit next to him. I said, 'Grandfather, before you set off for Kuttiyadi, with the household utensils, bedding and baggage, did you experience a feeling as if you were falling into a bottomless pit?'

Grandfather peered art me. Then said, 'Looks like you didn't sleep well last night. "I didn't sleep,' I said. 'I felt as if I was falling endlessly through the darkness. Does everyone who migrates feel this way?' 'I don't understand,' Grandfather said. 'I am going to migrate to Architect Joy's house forever. I haven't yet seen the house where I am to live for the rest of my life. I don't know whether it is situated on a hilltop or in a marshy place. I don't know whether it is a haunted house or not. I do know whether their ancestors had stolen others' wealth. If so, what if that curse falls upon the next generation?'

Sitting next to Grandfather, I aired all my fears and misgivings. Then said, 'Grandfather! I need to stay in Joy's house for at least a month before marriage. Only then will I be able to make bold to stay there, afterwards. I don't have the strength to journey into darkness, with my eyes shut.

Grandfather sat looking at me sorrowfully for quite some time. Then embracing me and with the accompanying smell of snuff, kissing my brow, he said, 'Dear child! I am on your side. But there is a difference between my time and your time. I am an old rationalist. I wish I had the strength to show you a way out. May God bless you!'

'Grandfather !' I exclaimed. 'Did you say "God"?'

Grandfather said, 'That's the last straw, you know.'

Doctor, I placed before my parents my demand that I should be permitted to stay in Architect Joy's house at least for a month before marriage. I added that, not only for this marriage proposal, but for any future proposals that came, this would be an essential condition. Today, peace, love and unity have ceased to exist in my home, doctor. My younger sisters have written remonstrating homilies to me. My elder brother has telephoned me threatening to put me in a mental hospital.

My mother's tears do not dry up. My father's sorrow has no end. Grandfather merely stares at the open book. Doesn't turn the pages. Only my grandmother who is a migrant twice over, is able to attend to the household chores like a robot, go to the church daily and also comfort me. Doctor, please help me. What must I do? Is there a way out for me? Can my demand be faulted? Am I a mental patient? Kindly advise me.

Thank you

Sincerely

Asha Matthew.

Satyakaam and Jaabaali

Amitabh

Bheempura was a Mang-Mahar Basti, just like any one of those quarters of the untouchables. It sheltered many boozers, guzzlers bootleggers, hirelings, and the likes. Mill workers, farm labourers, loafers, vagabonds, gamblers and rogues, and also some worthy men lived there. Some were the pilgrims of the holy Pandhari, some the devotees of the goddess Mari Mai. Also there were occultists, abortionists, flatterers, pimps, moneymakers, honoured ones, musclemen, weaklings, physical trainers and their chelas.

Those, who were capable of digesting the whole carcass of a buffalo within their own household, also lived there. Often, there would be slices of meat sun-dried in the courtyards of the houses of Hannya or Warlya. The stench would spread everywhere. Smelling a morsel of the rotten flesh, the crows would arrive. So would the kites and the vultures, and the dogs! Around all the places in Bheempura, filth and dirt abounded. The garbage lay dumped everywhere. It had hoards of bones stowed underneath. All kinds of dogs – white and black, scruffy and disease-ridden – would sniff at those bones, and stay there. They would shit and piss on the garbage dumps. So would the pigs. They would arrive there, if they were still hungry after guzzling the children's shit. Many of those places were the shitting grounds for the children. And why not? After all, who would care to clean the sides of the yards if the children defecated there? The morals from the books, teaching cleanliness on one's part to spare the neighbours from harassment, could not set foot here. Quarrels, abuses and fights were an everyday affair. Knives and daggers were drawn even for the flimsiest excuse, Murders were routine. Women would fight, pulling each others' locks, if a fowl from one's house went shitting in another's yard. Many husbands were quite used to taking their wives' places in each squabble, mauling the neighbour's wife. The sight of a bibulous husband battering his wife, or a quarrelsome wife whacking her husband's chest, was not taken as abnormal or incongruous.

Bheempura was a world on its own. Humans in this world were the insects and worms – that they sniffed and wriggled was the sole reason to regard them as alive, and not dead, that's all! No one thought of honour and insults and pride, no Sir, no one had! There was not much difference between the two-legged and the four-legged beasts. Yet, like a few bones still left in the beef, a few men with self-respect did live there. In fact, these men were a matter of pride for Bheempura – a thing of honour. Owing to them, Bheempura had kept moving ahead. Actually, no one ever knew when its usual trot changed into long strides later.

At the first siren from the old mill, Jaabaali rose from bed. Her only son, Satyakaam, was fast asleep beside her. He still held his pencil in his little fist. Jaabaali yawned, and stretched herself straight. She found a matchbox near the hearth and lit a kerosene lamp. That started her hectic routine for the day. In this Mang encampment, Jaabaali lived in a small shack of sticks and straws – a menage of crocks and clay-pots, where one earned with one's hand and ate out of bracts. She threw a few twigs of firewood under the three stones and blew hard on them to kindle the fire. Then, she put a pail of water on the stove to heat. Those blasted twigs – they would burn, and go out quickly, belching smoke. The smoke would rise and spread everywhere. It would reach her eyes, and hurt them. So, she sat near the stove to put in the fresh twigs. Her life had turned out to be just like this stove, she reflected. She had to keep on putting in the twigs of sorrow, just to keep alive. Only then could she expect a little warmth of happiness, and a flame of hope to rise. At times, sorrows and anguish wouldn't budge from her neck, like these wet twigs – no matter how hard she blew upon them, the fire would fail to rise. It brought a dizziness to her mind, and tears to her eyes. The whole future seemed to plunge into darkness.

Jaabaali was a widow. Her husband had died some nine or ten years before. He had gone into the forest of Koli to hunt wild boar. His spear had missed the target, and the hog had struck him frontally. After that, Jaabaali had decided to live as her husband's widow.

But her stomach was empty, so empty that it almost touched her backbone. And who can avoid hunger? Things would have been different if she were alone. But her old in-laws lived with her as her dependents. Within two years of her marriage, she had been widowed. So, everyone scoffed at her, calling her husband –gobbler. She frequented the forests of Chah-langadi or Chinchghat to gather firewood. Selling it, she could support her family. Sometimes, she took bundles of hay to the market, or went to work at the road-project, or at the mill. She believed she had no real reason to live after her husband. So, working in the forest, she would always put her hands in the ditches full of thorns and stones, hoping for a snake bite to rid her of her life. But neither did a serpent, nor a scorpion, ever oblige her.

Satam Saheb, from the mill, had started fresh recruitment in spinning section. Jaabaali got a job there. Better days were ahead now. Even her old in-laws felt so. They were ready to grant her their son's position, and to forget the events of the past. Yet, they kept a wary watch on Jaabaali, what with her sensuous body looking like a half-ripe mango fruit. A little delay in her coming back home, or some silly gossip reaching their ears, would make them put one thing against another, and accuse her. Jaabaali felt reduced – thought the gossip sweeter than the accusations.

At the mill, one had to reach before the third siren blew. The gates would close at the third siren, leaving the latecomers out. Many a time, this siren would start blaring before Jaabaali finished her household chores. She had to run to the mill to reach before the gates closed. Most women from Bheempura, as also from Nannashapura and Vithobapura, were often seen running like that towards the mill, to avoid the closing of the gates.

The path towards the mill went by the side of the village brook, crossing the front yard of the Maroti temple. On a platform against the temple, wrestler Martya Pahilwan, along with Dama Dangrya, Kisnya Telya and other loafers, always waited deliberately, doing push-ups. Eight or ten other brats from Dangaripura and Telipura, in underwear, would also be there, under the garb of physical work-outs. A few old men, returning from the stream-bed after defecation, would also stop there. All those men, sitting there, would leer at the women running towards the mill, and make dirty comments:

"Hey...look at her... how she runs... like a mare in heat."

"And here is the stud waiting for her..."

"Look... how her breast is bared."

"My ...my... what a big bust!"

"See her boobs jumping up and down..."

"Oh ...oh.. what a tight girl ... Should be fun putting the

cock in there..."

"Yeah ... like a soda water bottle..."

Such bawdy remarks were an everyday affair. The women would be mortified with shame and chagrin. Things were a little sober when the women had a male escort. But that was not possible each time.

That was the only route towards the mill. Jaabaali often dreaded being mauled by these hooligans.

One day, Martya did call her:

"Hey... Look how her boobs are shaking..."

"Why you ... don't you have women at home?"

"Yeah... a basketful of them , but what I need is you..."

At this, Martya climbed down from the platform. As he tried to grab her arm, Jaabaali struck him across the face, Enraged, he pulled away the sari from her bosom, and grabbed her blouse to rip it open. Only with luck was she saved that day, with a shout from Lakshya, who was rushing towards the mill from behind her.

But , Martya retaliated on the very third day. With no one else around, and Damya and Ramya at his side, he blocked her way. Rambhi, that wide-nose-sour-drinker of a girl who was with her, turned about and ran away hollering aloud. Martya held Jaaabaali and tore off her blouse. Then he lifted her and carried her inside the Maroti temple.

Jaabaali struggled to escape, like a goat under the butcher's knife, striking with her limbs and biting with her teeth – calling for anyone to come and rescue her. The devil Martya thrust his phallus into her mouth when she opened it to cry out. Then suddenly, he screamed as if a scorpion had stung him. He slapped her so hard in the face that her lips started bleeding through the cuts. A furious Martya picked up the burning wick from the temple lamp, and ripped off her clothes. He started scorching her naked skin with the flame on her breasts and her buttocks, hurling vile abuse at her.

"You fucking bitch ... bit me, didn't you? Now...take this..."

Her cries died out in thin air, with the piercing pain of the burns. Then, right in front of the scarlet god Maroti, Martya, Damya and Ramya raped her unconscious body.

Her old in-laws, when they heard of this, further waned in health. Eight days after, they both ended up in the graveyard. Jaabaali was left with no one at home. Good or bad as they were, they did provide a shade of support to her. And they had left her now. The whole sky seemed to cave in. Yet, there was one load off her mind. She was freed from the frequent insults flung by them like calling her "a tight-lipped harlot" or "a button-nosed coquette." That had stopped forever.

The house, and its door, had turned almost into a cowshed. She had tried with all her might, to build up her family but all that had evaporated now. So, the people were talking – what if they were? Can their lips be sewn up? She who spawns, gets stretched – she reflected. Where, were the people the other day? No mouth was opened, then. All just sat transfixed, watching the scene.

Fakra, also from the spinning section, had been going with her for some time. A widower himself, he had planned to marry her. Even he wouldn't soil his chest now, after that incident at the temple. But, one reaps what one sows. And, why blame others when one's own fate is at fault? So, Jaabaali passed the days, as they came.

Quite a hubbub was stirred up in Bheempura, and in the whole village, when Jaabaali gave birth to a child. It was difficult for a lass and a bereaved one at that – to live with honour in such a situation in Bheempura. Of course, each household had the same earthenware. So who would feel the sting at the arse. Yet, Warlya did perform a skit before the folks, singing, "The virgin breeds a tot, who's asleep under the cot."

Yet, taking all this rap, Jaabaali's son was growing, day by day. And the days truly went past. Who would keep on grating such a paltry incident for long? One day, the astute men of Bheempura took him under their wings. They consoled and supported her, so Jaabaali felt encouraged. Now, she strove hard to raise her son, Satyaakaam. She'd worked hard for over a week, and bought him a shirt and a pair of shorts. Both were a wee bit loose, but she calmed him saying they were fit for his growing body. She also bought him a slate and a pencil. It was the first of the month – the school would start today. She wanted to enrol Satyaakaam at the school.

Jaabaali touched the water in the pail to see if it was heated enough. Then she went to wake him up. He had slept with the slate and the pencil serving as pillow for him. The slate was pushed aside now, and the pencil held in his fist. She coaxed him awake and carried him to the gutter in the courtyard for his morning defecation. After washing his arse, she took him to the bathplace, and bathed him with soap and water, carefully scrubbing his skin with a stone. She dried him with the *pallu* of her sari and dressed him in the new shirt and shorts. Smearing a little coconut oil from a bottle, she carefully combed his hair. Then she got ready herself – combed her hair and wore the sari she had kept washed for this day.

The school yard was full of men and children, that day. Small boys in new dresses walked holding their mother's or father's fingers. Each one looked like a fresh flower just plucked from the tree. Many of them were known to Jaabaali. Hannya was there in the crowd. So were Ramchand, Tukya, Dawlya and Urkudya. The old women, like Nagayabudhi and Bavlayabudhi were also there, holding their grandsons' hands. Bheempura, Vithobapura, Nannashapura – almost all the camps seemed to have gathered there.

The headmaster Joshi sat there in his chair, He kept slicing betel-nut and munching it in his toothless mouth. He would ask this and that of the father of a child who stood at his table, and then write the name of the pupil in a large muster-book. Joshi master had worn a mark sandal-paste between his brows, and pagadi on his head, He wore a zari –bordered shawl across his shoulders. The wall behind him held the photos of Mahatma Gandhi and Jawaharlal Nehru. The wall in front was studded with pictures of Chatrapati Shivaji Maharaj and Ramdas Swami. The side wall had pictures of Dhyaneshwar and Tukaram. This same Joshi master, Jaabaali remembered, had grabbed at her when she had gone to deliver a roll of hay at his cowshed, a couple of years back. So – the same Joshi master was mustering the pupils' names.

"What name will you tell him, if asked?" she asked her son.

"Satyakaam," he answered, as taught.

"And the father's name?"

"Eh ... the father's ..."

"Forgotten so soon, have you?"

Which father – Jaabaali reflected – God knows how many have slept with me ... how can I tell him whose seed he belongs to?

"I haven't forgotten... the father's name is Jaabaali ," said her son.

"And the mother's?"

"The mother's is also Jaabaali"

She picked him up and kissed him again and again, holding him close.

"He'll ask why do you want to study... what'll you tell him?

"I'll say, I want to study and become as great as the reverend

Babasaheb," he answered, as always.

So, holding his hand, Jaabaali started walking briskly towards the school.

Kokila Mahari

Rabi Pattnaik

Why does an Indian black bird very often perch on a telegraph wire? Why does a crow caw, if a guest is to come?

Why does the koel sing secretly in the trees? Why has Kokila Mahari's life been so wasted and shattered?

There is certainly a reason for every act, an answer to every question. But the answers to all these questions have constantly eluded Kokila Mahari. When she was a child, she couldn't conceive these ideas even in the slightest of her imagination, and when she was a young woman she didn't have time at all for all these. Now in this old age she is haunted by these questions and she frantically seeks answers to them. Day by day she is more and more bent down with age. The more she is pressed down by the burden of life, the more agonisingly she searches for the answers. These answers seem to be the only key to her survival, a way of relief from this burden of life. Then only, she could have a sound and peaceful death.

Whose daughter is Kokila Mahari?

Is she the daughter of *Bada Panda*, the head priest of the temple of Lord Jagannath?

Of Talichhu Mahapatra, a temple official?

Of *Deula Karan,* the chief cook of Lord Jagannath?

Or of Bhikari Khuntia, the wrestler of the *sahi* where Kokila Mahari lives?

Whose daughter could she be? O, no, she is the daughter of no other than Jagannath, she is the daughter of Chanchala Mahari. Who can show the girl, who has lost the address of her father, her way to her husband's house? Many men have known their ways to Kokila's house but only her own man, her husband has not found the way.

That's why Kokila couldn't have the honour of being the daughter-in-law in a family. As she had been searching for a husband from among the crowd of her male visitors, she was not even aware when the time had elapsed.

What's the need for such a search now at this age of seventy?

Squatting clumsily on the front verandah of her house, she stares with a blank look into the street.

People say, Kalia, Lord Jagannath is her husband.

For about forty years she has tired herself singing and dancing before Kalia. But Kalia has not appeared even once before her and told her, 'Eh, Kokila, you are my wife.'

Kokila, Mahari, though a bed-mate of so many men, has been condemned to remain a spinster. She suffers from cataract in her eyes. Her hair has turned as grey as jute. Teeth have fallen. Toothless mouth and sunken cheeks. Loose wrinkled skin. Ears are almost deaf.

Someone shouted close to her ears, "Kokila *mausi*, someone has come to you."

Opening her cataract-affected eyes and looking dimly, she said, "Me? Who is that fellow trying to play jokes on me? Who will come to me at this age?"

Kokila Mahari is the only surviving representative of that lost community. Ramesh Pratihari has come to record her interview for his research project on Sri Mandir of Puri which will fetch him a Ph.D. degree in Oriya literature.

Ramesh said, "It's not a joke, *mausi*. I have come, in fact, to hear from you the story of your life. I like to know something about you."

The crone looked at him with disbelief and hummed, "So many years have passed but no one has ever cared to enquire about me. Strange that you are interested to know about me. But for Lord Jagannath's *khai bhog*, my life would have been finished."

Ramesh lives in Puri. Twenty-four years he has spent in Puri but this is for the first time that he has come to see Kokila Mahari's house. His friend Sadei Panda suggested to him, "Bhaina, it's difficult to bring the words out of her mouth. You have to spend some paise on *bhang* or opium. Her ears can't hear, nor can her eyes see. Only these intoxicants can move her to speak."

That day Ramesh came back. He went again the next day.

"*Mausi*, are you a resident of Puri?"

"Yes, certainly. Here I was born and here I will die."

"Can you tell me something about your childhood days?"

"Nothing, I can recollect nothing. Everything has been burnt and lost by this stupid mind. I am the daughter of Champa Mahari. My mother is ... Champa Mahari, do you understand my son? Even Bada Panda had to bow out of her way whenever he heard Champa Mahari coming. The king himself was mad to hear her song. And she was my mother, Champa Mahari."

The old woman's memory gets confused. No sense and order in what she says. Her tongue does not move well. Her voice is not clear. Half of what she says is not comprehensible. Ramesh has set the tape recorder on so that he can, later on, hear and make out what she says from the tape.

"I am the daughter of Champa Mahari. Do you think Kokila Mahari is my real name? It's a name given to me by His Highness the king himself. The day I sang *Ras Kallol* for the first time, my son, before His Highness – I don't know how old I was then, perhaps too tender to open my eyes – the court was full with people, courtiers, priests and pandits. When my song was over – I don't know how to describe it – the entire audience rose to applaud me. His Highness, just threw his chain of jewels over to me and addressed me Kokila which means koel; since that day I have been known as Kokila, Kokila

Mahari. My mother fondly named me Kalavati – Kalavati, hey ... hey ... that was burnt away in my mother's funeral pyre. Nobody has called me by that name since her death.

I had my lessons on dancing from Raghu Ostad who was a *gotipua* dance teacher. I also learnt songs from him. But my real teacher was my mother. She used to tell me, "When you sing before His Excellence Lord Jagannath, don't look into his eyes. Kalia will simply devour you. When you sing *Gita Gobind*, you have to give up all your shame. Sing with your eyes down and in a deeply engrossed mood. Forget everything then, lose yourself in a frenzy. Don't mind the rhythm, concentrate on the feeling only. Work yourself into an intense passion and imagine to yourself that that amorous Kalia playfully pulls the wear of your body and merges you in his body. He is that mischievous lover not the husband – the lover, the playboy in erotic games." My father's name, I don't know. Who could possibly be my father? ... O, it is Jagannath, Jagannath is my father. And Jagannath is my husband too. He makes his appearance before me sometimes as *Bada Panda*, sometimes as *Mahasuar*. Some other times as *Deula Karan*. At midnight he goes to bed, the sleeping hours of the Lord begin. The doors of the temple are closed tight. I often wonder how he comes out donning the same attire. In the dead of night he enters my house, plays sweet and colourful games of love with me the whole night and vanishes, when the dawn breaks.

The tree does not bear fruit. If it bears, he comes in the

same form and makes it disappear. At times he throws the fruit in the far off nest of a crow.

Before he her my mother once explained to me, "Kala, our Mahari life is the life of the koel. Male and female cranes, male and female doves, goose and gander, parrot and myna live as couples. Both the male and the female brood their eggs. Both bring up their baby birds. Only the koel is destined to live a life without husband and home. Male koels in groups climb at a time on a female koel and seduce her. After that they fly away leaving her alone in the lurch. The poor female koel lays eggs. But where is the nest to brood them in? So she carries the egg in her bill, helplessly moving about, seeking shelter here and there. Though she is a mother, she can't keep her baby with her. Who can she identify as the father of her baby? Who will bring her food, when she sits brooding the eggs? There is no husband in the koel's life, my dear Kala. All that she has is that mischievous lover who is without any attachment. It's for this anguish that the koel hides her face in the thick branches and leaves of the trees. Whom will she show her burnt and blackened face? She moves in the darkness of the thick foliage of the trees singing pitiful tales of her life. O' how sweet is her voice, everybody says. How beautiful! But who knows that amid the fullness of the spring, she is a forsaken and forlorn Mahari eternally pining for love?

A koel's child does not know her mother and father. A foundling, an illicit born! How dare she show her face? When she gains knowledge about life and becomes wise about the world, she almost dies from her own sense of shame and embarrassment. It's for this that she flies in the thick forest. An illegitimate child, forsaken by the society. Here in this life she is perhaps visited upon by the sin that she probably committed in some other life, ages after ages have not washed that sin away. The koel still carries that sin within her and for ages and generations together she has been making atonement for that. Who can predict when there will be the deliverance from this sin? Who has given this curse? Who has engraved this eternal sin in the fate of the bird of this species?

My dear Kala, this curse is written into our fate. Who can violate it at all? For such a long time, for hundreds of years we have been singing the songs of our woe before Kalia, but he has not yet granted us freedom from the bondage of that sin. Who else, then, is there to deliver us from this wheel of suffering? Don't feel depressed, my dear; banish from your mind thoughts about husband and family. If one brings to one's life battered by disillusionment will fade away. Even in youth one rots away with anguish. It is better to abandon yourself to your fate and deed and enjoy as much pleasure as you can snatch from life. Spend your life laughing and playing, singing and dancing before Kalia so long as you can. Perhaps Kalia will liberate the Maharis – if not the Maharis of your time, then may be, the Maharis who will come after you."

"With the words of my mother constantly ringing in my

mind, I have already spent seventy years of life. Some years with happiness, some with unhappiness. Now there is no pain or joy."

Ramesh Pratihari spoke loudly, "*Mausi*, nowadays there is no Mahari in the temple. That system has been abolished long since. Your prayer has been heard by God."

But Kokila Mahari could not hear anything, for she was deaf and also by that time the opiate sleep had come over her. She quietly rolled on the verandah and slept.

The Deadline

Lal Singh

The deceased was known by a variety of names – Sat Pal, S.P. Anand, Satti and Pali. When I stepped into this house as a bride, he was my brother-in-law by way of familial relationship. As a young boy, he played with the ball in the verandah, sulked over trifles, and refused to eat the vegetables cooked for meals. By way of a natural relationship, however, he was my son, my brother and my lover.

Today was Satti's first death anniversary. Brahmins were fed, donations were given and whatever token still remained of him in the house was given away in charity. Everything was done for the peace of this motherless boy's family –for me, his Bhabhi, a mother figure to him, his noble brother, and his paralytic, bedridden father. I do not know what happens to the soul of the dead. Is it reincarnated? Does it still haunt this house or the house of his fiancee? Perhaps it hovers on the parapet of the room on the terrace in Santosh's house. Santosh is married to Satti's cousin. I must speak to Anand Sahib to go on a pilgrimage to Pehowa. The soul of the deceased will then rest in peace. At least Pitaji will be at peace.

After a day of inconsequential discourse by the relatives and friends, of endless rounds of tea, I have manged to steal a moment to myself. Listless and drained, I look back and wonder at the turn of events God ordained for us. Satti lived the last nine months so intensely that they crowded out the first twenty-three years of his young life.

But only Satti knew or perhaps I do know how he lived through the months after Dr. Puri diagnosed his throat cancer. Whatever I had heard or read about cancer patients was half-truth. The whole truth was what we actually experienced and lived.

After his graduation and a year long spell of unemployment, Satti got employment. But before the year ended, the persistent irritation in his throat was diagnosed as cancer. When he gave us the report, Dr. Puri, a maternal uncle of mine, broke into beads of sweat all over his bald head. Putting his hands on our shoulders, he said, "Satti will not live for more than six months. His cancer is terminal. If you must spend money, spend it on charity. I will, if you like, prescribe some medicine."

How could Dr. Puri know our pain and helplessness? We were constantly troubled by the knowledge that we could not save a dying man. That evening I handed the passbook of our joint bank account to my husband. It recorded a balance of Rs 17,000. "Why do we need to save this amount?" I asked him.

About a year after our marriage, I gave birth to a daughter. It was a caesarean delivery. But I could not suckle her even for six months. God gifted her to us and He took her back.

I gave up my job after the loss of my daughter. For whom do we need to amass wealth? Anand Sahib earned well at the bank. Besides, Satti was too young to take care of his clothes and studies on his own. Pitaji also needed to be looked after. He could barely manage to climb down from his bed, drag himself to the toilet, and crawl back to the bed. Nor could he change his shirt without assistance. Besides, his speech was and still is incoherent. Before my marriage, his mumblings were understood by my mother-in-law. After her death, it became my sacred duty to read his lips.

On our return from Dr. Puri's clinic, we stood at the door of Pitaji's room clutching the report. He looked up expectantly for fruit but we could not bring ourselves to meet his eyes. We hastily withdrew into our room.

Satti had still not returned from the office. 'How do we tell him?' Anand Sahib mused. Deeply troubled, he broke down. His hands hid his eyes. I could no longer hold back my tears but I hurriedly brushed them away. I assured my husband that I would break the news to Satti. I felt that in the absence of my mother-in-law, it was my responsibility to tell him the truth. I am the mother in this household. If I surrender to tears, Satti will be inconsolable. Pitaji will also be upset. How can we survive then?

At night when Anand Sahib went for his walk and Pitaji fell asleep after dinner, I talked to Satti. The conversation started casually about cancer patients. It moved to the question of how cancer patients struggle to salvage what remains of their lives, and how they cannot choose but accept death with resignation and without grief. Finally I broached the subject of Dr. Puri's diagnosis as a dreaded possibility.

Satti's face betrayed little fear but his smile froze. When he expressed his desire to meet Dr. Puri for a consultation, I handed him the report. The report, however, did not make any mention of cancer. Besides, the medical terminology made little sense to a layman. He threw a fleeting glance at the report, then folded it and put it away. He coughed nervously, got up, and retired to his room.

I stood watching him shuffle the contents of his table for a while. Then he came out of his room and stood on the verandah, gazing across at the flowers growing in the bed next to the gate. I felt that the wheel of death had been set into motion. When Anand Sahib returned at night, he lay down, lit a cigarette and announced his decision, "We will go in for treatment. Numerous cancer patients have survived for as many as ten years." He had obviously been talking to his friends. "Yes, why not?" was all I could say in response. The thought that even a pinch of sacred ash blessed by a holy man has the power to cure terminal diseases flitted across my mind.

I took out Rs 2000 and gave them to my husband. The

sight of money seemed to irritate him. The angry tone of his voice was a fresh reminder that funds and treatment were my responsibility. I apologised to him and walked to Satti's room. Satti had fallen asleep. In the morning when I brought him tea, Satti was still sleeping. His long and curly hair fell over his forehead. His luminous brow, the thick sketched eyebrows, and the soft hair on the bridge of his nose had always fascinated me. It is generally believed that people blessed with great beauty die young. Something stirred within me. I swept his hair away and kissed his brow.

When I first stepped into this house as a young bride, Satti was a small and playful boy. An aunt from Ambala caught hold of him and placed him in my lap. It could be custom or an invocation to God to bless me with sons. But I understood it to be an unspoken injunction that I was mother to him.

In my parental home, I used to assist Subhash, my younger brother, with dressing for school. I started doing the same for Satti.

Satti woke up and smiled at me. But instantly gloom spread across his face. Perhaps he sensed the sadness lurking behind my smile. Anand Sahib came into the room and stood by my side. Unable to look Satti in the eye, he turned his face towards the window and assured Satti, "Don't worry. The disease is curable. Today we will go to the C.M.C. Hospital at Ludhiana."

At the hospital, Dr. Joseph offered very little comfort. He said, "It lies in God's hands to cure. Man can only try the treatment. Let us begin in the name of God."

After a month's course, Satti's condition seemed worse than before. We consulted a sadhu at Ferozepur and then a much touted hakim whose medicine was made from turmeric.

Treatment continued and money flew like paper into thin air. We discovered a *vaid* at Kurukshetra but as a last resort, we took Satti to P.G.I. at Chandigarh.

I made it a point not to leave Satti alone. We played cards, carrom and other games or we watched a movie. Satti licked his thumb and forefinger before dealing the cards. At meals he dipped his morsel into my bowl of vegetables. When he dared me to a wager, he smacked his hand against mine. Panic surged inside me.

I went to Dr. Puri for advice. He assured me that cancer was not infectious but it was good to take precautions. I laughed in relief but deep down fear still gripped me. At times my love for him so overpowered me that I forgot all fears.

One day we went to watch an English movie. When we returned home and started to climb the stairs to the terrace, Satti gallantly offered me his arm in imitation of the celluloid hero. In the same style, I held his hand and kissed it when we reached the last step. A strange look flashed in his eyes. I sat in the chair seemingly unconcerned but watched, in the mirror of the almirah, the shifting expressions on his face. The flush was fast fading into pallor.

"What's the matter? Why are you so pensive?" I questioned

him in a tender voice and put my hand on his shoulder. He buried his head in my lap and burst into tears. I caressed his head and back, held him tightly in my arms, and exclaimed, "You are my precious life!" With a sigh, he responded in English, "I am losing my life."

His words stabbed my soul. It was the first time he had spoken of death. I kissed him on the forehead and answered in English, "I dedicate my life to you, my dear."

Fear robbed Satti of sleep. The knowledge that he lay sleepless at night chased away our sleep too.

One night, around half past two, I heard someone call out. I thought Satti was asking for water. I scrambled to open the connecting door and found him lying prone on his stomach. His face was sunk into the pillow and his body was sprawled out on the quilt. How could he be thirsty on such a cold night? What storms were raging inside him? I sat close to him on the bed, ran my hand over his head, and asked, "Can't you sleep?" He replied, "No, I can't. I have been tossing and turning for two hours now."

I gave him a sleeping pill. Anand Sahib had started taking "Campose" and at times even I needed it. "Bhabhiji , I need a drink," Satti muttered softly. He did not want his brother to overhear his request. He could not bear to look me in the eye.

"Fine! Let me first consult the doctor. Do try to sleep for now." I pulled the quilt over him and returned to my bed. For the rest of the night, I lay wide awake.

The next day, after completing the daily chores, I went to Dr.Puri. His prompt reaction was, "Give him whatever he wants. Feed his soul. Learn to accept what has to be. What is the use of brooding over the inevitable end?"

The conviction that Dr. Puri's platitudes may be comforting for others but not for us hastened my exit from the clinic. How could Dr. Puri know that it killed us by slow degrees to watch a young man caught in the jaws of death, that the fear of death had seeped into every brick of our house, and the shadow of death had settled on every face? Pitaji was the only member of the family who was blissfully unaware of the reality. But even he scanned our anxious faces. I was utterly lost for words when Pitaji asked me one day, "Why are you always morose? Why doesn't Satti go to work? Where do you take him?"

Once I almost confessed to him, "Pitaji, your beloved son has little time to live. We take him to all those places which are renowned for the treatment of cancer."

Satti came home drunk one evening. He staggered towards his room on unsteady feet but collapsed on the threshold. When I helped him to his feet, he draped his arm around my neck, subsided into the bed, pulled away my dupatta and covered his face with it. One half of the dupatta still clung to my head and the other half shrouded his face. He was in tears, haunted perhaps by the spectre of death.

How does a young man come to terms with unfulfilled

desires on the brink of death? The thought shook me to the core.

After about an hour and a half, when Anand Sahib went to see how Satti was doing, he found Satti vomiting. The vomit carried traces of blood. I hurriedly mopped the mess, and ensured that Anand Sahib did not notice the spots of blood.

The next day was Sunday. As was the routine, we made preparations for the *havan*. Satti seemed distracted. In the past he participated in the *havan* with complete devotion. He recited the *Sandhya* in the evening. His brother and I religiously chanted the mantra *Jeevan Shradha Shattam* – May life bloom for a hundred years. Propped against the pillar, Pitaji, as always, simply listened to the chanting.

Satti lit the fire in the *havan kund* with an obvious lack of interest. At the end of each mantra he chanted *swaha* and sprinkled *ahuti* into the fire. But halfway through the recitation he pulled back to lean against the wall. His eyes were closed.

Satti came home in the evening after watching a movie. He paced restlessly about the house for a while, swallowed his medicine, and started to go out again but I stopped him. I poured a peg from a quarter bottle of English whisky stored in the cupboard and placed the drink on the table. A smile spread across his face. I said, "Drink if you must but in your own house. Not in your uncle's. God knows what junk food you eat at his house."

To be honest, I did not like his dining with relatives or

drinking with their wayward sons. Nor did I want to be subjected to the sarcastic comments which I knew would follow. As it is , Santosh, their daughter-in-law, didn't mince her words! Moreover, her behaviour was not above reproach. God knows with whom she remained closeted for long hours in the room on the terrace. By the time I came back to the room after completing the kitchen work, Satti had drained the drink. He asked, "Bhabhiji , when will Virji return?"

"He will return in the morning. On his way back, he plans to visit his aunt at Amhala," I told Satti.

His eyes on the drink, Satti asked me somewhat diffidently, "Is there any more liquor in the house?"

My first impulse was to lie to him. Excessive drinking could be harmful. Then I thought what more could go wrong in the two and a quarter or, at the most, two and a half months left for him to live? "Yes, there is more but I won't give it to you," I teased. His disappointment touched my heart. It seemed sinful to deceive or to lie to a dying young man. His brow and even the soft hair on the bridge of his nose seemed to wrinkle into a frown.

I got up to open the cupboard. When he came and stood close to me, I felt that his breathing was frayed. I gave him what was left of the quarter bottle. He took the bottle and thanked me with a kiss on my shoulder. He murmured something but his words eluded me. A shiver flowed like a wave through my body.

I sat down in a chair opposite him, and gazed at him. He took another glass and poured a drink for me. I did not know how he could divine what was in my heart. Is it possible that a dying man's sixth sense is sharper than ever before?

Despite my impassioned protests, he held me tightly and poured the liquid down my throat as though he was forcing me to drink a bitter medicine. Twice in my life I had tasted liquor. Once before marriage, I had a drink at a friend's house. It left me strangely cold. The second time I drank with Anand Sahib to the point of getting drunk. The experience was bitter-sweet. The morning after I had such a massive hangover that I have not touched liquor since then. That day, however, I did not have the heart to refuse Satti. In fact I could not deny Satti anything any more. He simply had to ask.

I served Satti his dinner. His hands were shaking uncontrollably. As he broke the morsels, dipped them into the bowl of vegetables, and carried them to his mouth, his eyes were transfixed on my face. Suddenly he stopped eating and moaned in a thin voice, "Bhabhiji !" He spread his arms on the table and buried his face in them. I ran my hand over his head and gently said. "Come, lie down." When he looked up, his face was flushed. His eyes were also bloodshot. I understood what he wanted but my mind was slowly growing numb. What does Hindu religion have to say about a tormented soul which leaves the body after death still hungry for the love of a woman?

I assisted Satti to his feet and almost carried him to the bed. My own feet hardly touched the ground.

As I was about to turn away after tucking him into the quilt, he caught hold of my sari and pleaded, "Bhabhiji, help me to meet Nirmal just once."

A cry convulsed my body. "How can I possibly bring Nirmal to you, my dear? She has not come to see you even once."

Overwhelmed with my own helplessness I sat down on the bed, kissed him and gently lifted his head to nestle it in my lap. He put his arms around me and held me tightly like a frightened child clinging to his mother.

I froze for a tiny fraction of time but after that we were no longer conscious of who we were. At that moment was I his Bhabhi, his sister, his mother or his wife?

His face loomed over me –the luminous brow, the bushy eyebrows, and the thinly drawn lips. Perhaps what I saw was not his face but his body which was blazing like molten lead. Or perhaps, I was face to face with his soul – pure, naked and defenceless. Our souls were naked but our bodies were covered. I felt that a *havan* was in progress. Each offering fanned the fire and the flames leapt higher with every chant of "*savaha*".

When the hymn of peace was over, Satti, completely drained, sank into deep slumber. Lying by his side, I ran my eyes over his innocent face. His face reminded me of the young boy for whom I used to stand for long hours on the roof of our house so that I could catch a glimpse of him. I got up, kissed him on the bridge of the nose, pulled the quilt over him, and returned to my bed. My mind was besieged with questions: "What have we done? Are we to be condemned to hell?" I felt that whatever I had learnt from the holy scriptures was not true. Truth is what circumstances compel us to know and to experience. Under certain circumstances, even murder is not a crime.

The next day was a Sunday. Anand Sahib returned around seven in the morning. Perhaps he did not want to disturb the pattern of a Sunday morning *havan*. Perhaps he was superstitious about the ritual. I woke up Satti so he could have his bath and perform the *havan*.

We sat around the *havan kund* – Anand Sahib on my right and Satti on my left. Across from us sat Pitaji, reclining against the pillar for support. I offered water in four directions around the *havan kund*, prayed for the strength of the body, and sprinkled water over Satti and myself. It was ironic that we were praying for a strong body and a long life of hundred years but Satti was left with no more than thirty days to live.

After the *havan*, I followed Anand Sahib to the bedroom and asked, "What does the *vaid* at Kurukshetra say?" "What can he say? He believes cancer is incurable so we may or may not use his medicine. Anyhow, I have brought medicine for fifteen days."

Flames leapt in the *havan kund* placed in the verandah. Pitaji was still sitting against the pillar. His eyes flickered from Satti to the fire and then turned to the sky. I could hardly breathe.

Anand Sahib suggested, "Why don't we take Satti to the P.G.I. at Chandigarh? They have devised a new treatment. The patient's thigh is scratched and splattered with the medicine. The doctors observe the patient for a week. Radiotherapy is also part of the treatment. How much money is left?"

"There is enough to take care of expenses. You may decide as you please," I said and turned to the kitchen. My mind was full of questions. "Who knows how much medicine has to be bought? From where will it come? Where and when is Satti destined to die? What will he gain by going to Chandigarh? But then, what will he lose?"

When Satti returned home in the evening after wandering around the whole day, he was restless. He took me upstairs and kept talking in a rambling fashion. I sensed that he wanted to drink but his brother's presence in the house inhibited him. I took the liquor bottle to him and arranged for whatever else he needed.

Anand Sahib went to the market to buy porridge. As though on cue, Satti tumbled down the stairs. He entered the kitchen and stood behind me. He was breathing hard. I turned to face his blazing eyes and touched his burning eyebrows. He pleaded, "Please kiss me."

I swept his hair off his forehead, held him in my arms and kissed him. For a while I stood holding him to my bosom. But I was nagged by the thought that the seeds of sin are sown when we are prompted to act for selfish reasons. I tried to pull away from Satti but he clung to me. I did my best to teach him some sense, put the fear of Anand Sahib in him, and pushed him away with a vague promise. Only then did he go out to sit on the verandah. It was for this reason that I had to sack the girl employed for mopping and cleaning the house. And for this very reason, I had not allowed him to visit Santosh, his cousin's wife.

After dinner Anand Sahib went for a walk. Satti began throwing tantrums like a child. Despite my pleas, he switched off the bedroom light.

When his desire was fulfilled, he started to doze. I felt as though my dying son was resting by my side. I offer him my breast brimming with milk but he lacks the strength to suck...

When I regained focus, I found myself holding Satti as a mother holds her baby – suckling and snoozing all at once.

I rushed to the bathroom, brushed my teeth, and rinsed my mouth. Fear gripped me. Initially I used to cover my face to protect my lips but his insistence and my own weakness crumbled my defences. I forgot that he was a cancer patient.

In the afternoon I rushed to Dr. Puri's clinic. I spun a tale of an affair Satti was having with the newly-employed maid. The doctor was reassuring, "Don't worry. There is no fear of infection." My apprehensions, however persisted.

A horde of our relatives lived in Chandigarh but we decided against staying with any of them. It didn't seem right to impose a patient upon them. We rented a room with an attached kitchen in Sector 15. The house was quite close to the hospital. After the hospital rounds, the two of us – Deor Bharjai – cooked our meals and played cards. In the evening we went for a walk or explored the shopping centres. Satti was happy in the crowds. I bought him whatever he liked. He selected and bought a wide range of cosmetics for me. Once he set his heart on buying me a scarf. I simply loathed the deep red, blue and yellow streaked scarf but his whim and persistence compelled me to wear the scarf on the way back home. I wore it even to bed that night.

The cold weather had nearly disappeared but Satti preferred to close the doors and windows at night. The hunger to feast his eyes on a woman's body had still not abated. Sometimes his eyes were fixed on me but his mind was lost in thought, he would bury his face between my breasts and burst into tears.

At the hospital when people asked me, "Is he your brother?" I responded, "Yes, he is." If someone asked me, "Is your son?" my answer was again in the affirmative. But if someone asked me, "How is he related to you?" I was lost for words. What could I say? In Chandigarh, he lived as my husband, the lord and master of my body.

Woman was no longer a mystery to him. Nor was love making more than a mechanical routine. With each passing day, his body shrivelled either due to radiology or to his mental condition. It was hard to ascertain the reason. His zest and will power started to weaken. Even his interest in food and clothes disappeared. At times he took to drinking. Sometimes, he meditated or recited *shlokas* from the Gita in a loud voice. I used to wonder, "How can his repeated recital of the *shloka Nayeenam Chhindanti Shastrani* – No weapons can pierce the soul – comfort him? Does he care whether the soul is indestructible and eternal?"

We came home after completing the treatment at P.G.I. Satti found it increasingly difficult to eat even the porridge. Sometimes his condition took a turn for the worse. He could hardly breathe. The whole day long he lay on the bed and stared at the gate. At times fear possessed him. His arms and legs, or the entire body convulsed in the same way a child trembles in the throes of a nightmare. Sometimes his hands and his lips shook uncontrollably. I made him tea or coffee, sat with him and pressed his hands. He would regain his composure in time. His obsession with the gate, however, persisted.

One day Pitaji asked me, "How is Satti? What does the doctor at P.G.I. say?" It was clear to me that Satti's aunt had visited the house in my absence and divulged the news of Satti's illness to Pitaji. My silence seemed to upset him. His lips started trembling—a typical mark of anger or hurt in the Anand clan. His reaction was intense. I confessed to Pitaji that Satti was dying. My words hung in the air. I picked up the utensils and hurried into the kitchen. I could not bear to show him my tears nor could I see his tears. His murmur followed my receding back, "Sell the land in the village."

At evening tea, Pitaji beckoned Satti to a chair opposite him. He stared at Satti, mumbled a few words, folded his hands and closed his eyes as he did when he was praying. I signalled to Satti to leave Pitaji to his prayers.

One day Satti sat smoking on the verandah. I was working in the kitchen. His screams drew me out. He had fallen off the chair. The cigarette lay smouldering on the floor. I helped him to his feet. Satti moaned, "Bhabhiji, I can't breathe." I rubbed *desi ghee* on his throat.

The deadline had finally arrived. That night was to be his last. I could not sleep a wink. Anand Sahib recited *Gayatri Path*. Satti had fallen asleep. I went twice to his room to check on him.

Suddenly his breathing was still. I held my breath and froze. Then I pulled myself up and ran into his room. Gently I lifted a corner of the coverlet. His breathing reassured me but his face looked wan. I leant over Satti and my eyes ran over his face. Once it used to be red like a rose.

Back in my room, I checked the time. It was quarter to midnight. I gave Anand Sahib a sleeping pill but he refused. The night – the deadline set by Dr. Puri – was finally over.

In the morning Anand Sahib performed the *havan*. In deference to Pitaji's wishes, a large quantity of grain and many clothes were given away in charity on behalf of Satti.

In the afternoon once again, Satti fell off the chair. Luckily

Anand Sahib was at home. We picked Satti up and rushed to him Dr. Puri's clinic. God knows how and what Dr. Puri did but Satti started to breathe normally and effortlessly. In ten days, much to the surprise of even his doctor, Satti made a complete recovery.

Once again he was as healthy as a horse. He ate everything and loafed around. He took to indulging himself in ways I found distasteful because they filled me with shame for both of us. Quite often he spent time alone with Santosh in the terrace room, drank with his good-for-nothing cousins, and generally behaved like a ruffian. Despite my protests, he rummaged through my purse for money. When we made love, his eyes did not shine with the love we once knew. I felt as though a debauch lay waiting to possess me, as though to take anything from anybody on loan or on demand was his right. Satti transformed into a rogue who fed off others. It was not brute force but cancer which goaded him to behave like a parasite. Cancer was slowly killing him and, in turn, Satti was killing us.

After a month and a half, once again, his condition took a sudden turn for the worse. When streaks of blood surfaced in his phlegm, Satti was shaken to the core. Anand Sahib was also apprehensive. I forced medicines on him all over again. Defeated and exhausted, Anand Sahib mused one evening, "Who knows how long this hell..." "Why don't you pray? All our sorrows will blow over," I suggested. But I did not know whose hell he was talking about – Satti's, Pitaji's or his own? I wanted to ask him, "If what you are experiencing is hell, what am I living through?"

We never knew where Satti wandered during the day but evening invariably drew him back home. As dusk fell, fear seemed to consume him. At night, he lay in bed and read holy books. His face was always turned to the main gate. During the day whenever he sat on the verandah, his eyes watched the gate.

Sometimes his face radiated so much calm that it surpassed the serenity on the face of the devout. At times his restlessness possessed him to such a degree that he was in a desperate rush to go somewhere or for someone to come. He was like a traveller who restlessly paces up and down the platform as he waits for a train. Or perhaps he was more like a traveller who, having missed the train, sits forlorn on the deserted platform.

One day Satti sat meditating with legs crossed and eyes closed. I stood facing him. He opened his eyes, shut them again, folded his hands and bowed his head.

Lord knows how but the night before his death, Satti intuitively knew that the end had come. He beckoned me to his bed. I bolted the connecting door and sat close to him. On his pleading, I lay down by his side. For a long while, his eyes lingered over my face. Then tears flooded and shadowed his eyes. Immediately I clasped his face to my heart. "What is it, my child?" My question tumbled out with force and urgency.

He closed his eyes as though he was meditating. Next morning, he refused the bed tea. He took his bath, lit the incense and started to pray. Hardly had he recited the opening mantras when the prayer book slipped from his hands and he collapsed on the floor. A scream shrilled through my body. Anand Sahib was shaking as he ran towards us. It was all over. The end dreaded by all of us – Satti. Anand Sahib and I – was here.

Today marks the first anniversary of Satti's death. I am still groping for an answer to the question, "What was Satti to me?"

The Whip

Chandra Prakash Deval

Like so many other things, a whip, too, gets tired after being in constant use for long. Isn't it true?" Mannu was anxious to ask his Ma, who still was unable to overcome the pain in her back...

'But then it leaves one wounded and skin stripped before being withdrawn.

What a long time it takes for the wound to heal. Not years of course.

'Even if it takes years, that is good my son!' Alert yet upset, holding the finger of her son, she went on. Utter darkness. The road , too is dark.

'Where are we going Ma? Where to?' asked Mannu.

'If there were any destination, I would have told you.'

'Then will we go on for ever as we are doing now?'

Yes my son! At least up to the time our legs and sense of fortitude do not wear out.

'But to where will this lead us?'

'Be silent. We are to go out of the reach of that whip'

'How long is the reach of the whip, Ma?'

'Right from the first man born in the creation of this Universe to the present generation of men.'

This pertains to time.

Whenever something unusual happens in the life of a woman, then these damned beings...

'Time and space get mixed up. My son, therefore whatsoever the measure be, the distance remains the same.'

Out then, Ma my arithmetic...

'It is shallow ... the meaning of your arithmetic will also change when you grow old.' Once again she wiped her tears. She stopped. Then began. Felt the whipped out skin on her back. Then gazed at the road spread out before her, trying to cross over it and for ever, Walk she did not, It was running.

Almost.

'Ma, does it pain a lot?' asked Mannu weeping.

'No, not at all. However a pain of some other sort haunts my being.'

'What sort, Ma?'

'You won't understand. You're too small.

'Let us go to our village, Ma! There is the jamun-tree. I will make a paste of its crushed leaves and will apply it on your wounds. And the black soil of the Sukh-Sagar pond, besmeared on your body, will certainly soothe your pain. I will fan you with the cardboard of my drawing file.'

'This road too will surely take us to some village.'

'But, there, how will Suraj and Shanta be found? asked Mannu.

'What have we to do with the Sun? We will have to travel a long distance and go still beyond... and my son, peace is not there for us... we are fated thus,' said Ma thoughtfully.

'No, no Ma, I was talking about my friends in the village.'

'The village, our village is lost somewhere, sonny.'

'Then, let us go to my nana's home', suggested Mannu.

'That, too, slipped away the day when we had found our village. And now even if it is there, what shall we do there. What will we say to them? I cannot answer queries like why and how we have come', Ma exhaled.

Ma was getting breathless. Her breast heaved, She had been walking too briskly. She did not feel like saying anything.

They were both silent for some time. It seemed that neither the night, nor the road, nor the journey would ever come to an end.

Along with them the whip's circumference too seemed to increase. 'My son, the whip is as long the atrocious night. It lashes and takes away the skin, Pray, let no one fall a victim to it. Let not the flap touch you either, my son!' Nobody could know what Ma was whispering between her lips. Mannu did not hear it properly. He was simply trying to keep pace with Ma's steps, with his sweating finger, slipping away from her fist in the cold night. Silence crept in. They went on in the calm of night. Time clicked on...

'Ma, when I grow older, I will burn the wire of the hot iron.'

'Then papa...?' he ultimately decided after pondering over some solution for some time.

'Sonny, burnt out wire does not mean a burnt out whip, 'Ma cut him short.

'I will burn all the ropes, then'

'Even then, the whip cannot be destroyed.'

'I will burn all the leather of the world. Then?'

'Then, the whip will be made of other things.'

'Of what?'

'From jute or the grass-rope!'

'I will put to ashes all the jute and the grass too.'

Ma was struck. Her heart shook. Held off his hand and said in anger and fear, 'I will not allow you to do such atrocious things when you grow older. Keep silent. Don't talk nonsense. Have you taken upon yourself the responsibility of burning, the whole world? You are showing your true colours right now.' She scolded Mannu.

'Forgive me, Ma. I will not do any thing like that. But you too wish to destroy the whip.'

'The whip does not have one form only.'

'Then?'

'It is the name of fury. Whichever way that fury moves and at that moment whatever comes to one's grip, that very thing becomes a whip . The wheel of a chariot and any round-shaped thing becomes a *sudarshan chakra;* in a moment it is the wristlet of Bhasmasur, given to him by an innocent Shankar like me. Then Shankar himself is to run around in order to save his life, as we are doing. The whip is invisible so too is its lashing,. It cuts you to pieces somewhere within. There is no balm, no cure, to its lashing my son! Yes, it is certain that as soon as the whip comes to one's grip, it takes away all reason. And the man without reason is a dead body. Like lightning in the sky violence in him erupts and destroys many things. For instance, love and the sense of belonging are burnt in its initial flames. And the man becomes a fused cracker. Once broken, nothing can come together, neither relations, nor glass. All such things shatter to pieces and the broken pieces pierce and pinch throughout one's life. Ugh, a person can neither live more or die in peace...'

And all of a sudden she thought of death. Suicide... no.. no, it is worse than death ... suicide is the name condemning an innocent person who is no more to live... She suppressed this horrible idea and rushed on.

'Ma, what have you been saying? I could not follow,' said Mannu.

'It's good you don't understand.'

'Then why did you grow young?'

'Yes, it was my mistake...' She spoke as if saying to herself.

'See, Ma, we've reached the station. The lights are visible.'

'There are so many stations and platforms in the journey of life and age stops nowhere,' she sighed and again said 'yes it seems we're near the station.'

'Let us go there, Ma.'

'Yes, after all we have to go somewhere,' And then she thought for a while and said to herself, 'How far can man run away from himself? Who asked you for this life of a woman? O God! Why did you create woman? But Omniscient God, you too are not at fault; after all you too are a male. O Natnager who faced the thrashing leg of Bhrigu, had you borne the lashing whip? Then and only then you would have been something, some real incarnation. If there had been the whip and its lashing in your world... no... no, it would have caused havoc. Radha and Rukmani too would have met me here rushing towards the station and you, O Lord, would have become helpless and utterly restless in your celestial court and would have wasted scores of matchsticks in lighting a cigar. But your heavenly ego is hurt if you try to repent in a proper way. Then she consoled herself saying, 'Forget all these musings. These are simply the ways to console oneself. They are false notions on the scriptures. But can an agonised soul ever be calmed? At such a juncture, nothing is real, no God, no incarnation. The only real thing is the station and the lights thereof, and the finger of her child in her fist. This bone-biting cold is real. This dark road is real. The dark night is real. And the pain within. And the man, and the world. And the only unreal, falsehood is the woman and that too, a mother.

She halted and Mannu said, 'See, Ma, Tiger too has been following us.'

'Yes, my son only a dog can see Yamraj and his buffalo and the whip in his hand. People say so.'

'Does Yamraj too keep a whip?' asked Mannu.

'Perhaps, the dogs weep and howl therefore, wherever they see him.'

'Ma, let us go in. I am scared of such things.'

'Fear, is yet another name of the whip. It slashes the soul and hurts a great deal.

I could not understand soul and inner pain, perhaps!

Hurry Ma, the signal is down, the train is due. We will sit in the train and will go to wherever it takes us. And then we will buy a huge whip from the other corner of the world and then will come back in the same train, to the same station... We will reach our home and will whip the hands which hold the whip, and then no one will ever dare to hold the whip. '

And then Ma gave him a slap and wept and cried and wept

and wept. Mannu was taken aback, a film of sudden darkness filled his vision and then her own cry got lost in the howling of Tiger. The train had left without whistling. It was creeping, crawling away.

Sometimes

Ishwar Chander

It was really a surprise meeting. They had run into each other after almost eight years. They were too dazed for words and for quite some time, stood merely looking at each other. When the surprise ebbed, they spoke a few words and then went into a nearby restaurant. A seven-year-old boy accompanied the woman.

They occupied a table near the one occupied by an Anglo-Indian couple. The boisterous laughter of the couple drew their attention. The woman caught the eye of her companion and smiled. Said she, "They not only speak English, but also laugh in English." The joke probably was lost on the man. She didn't mind. She knew that the man was devoid of a sense of humour. He had always been like that, even when she had met him eight years ago.

She preferred to remain vague to start with. Thumbing over the pages of the menu, she casually asked, "When did you arrive in this place?"

"Three days ago."

"Oh! I see. What brought you here, anyway?"

He meditated for a moment and said, "The monotonous and dreary life in Madras. It had been getting on my nerves for some time. I thought of having a change of environment and came away."

He brought out a pack from his pocket, took a cigarette and lit it. He placed the pack and the matchbox on the table.

"I thought you would have changed over the years. But you haven't."

He looked at her quizzically, trying to understand the import of her remark. He asked, "Changed in what way?"

"You didn't offer me a cigarette. Didn't courtesy demand it?" She picked up the pack, took out a cigarette and lit it.

With a surprised look the man watched her smoke. Before he could speak, the waiter came to their table.

"What would you like to have?" The man asked turning his head to the woman.

"Oh! no," the woman said. "Presently you are a visitor here and so you are my guest. Do I sound formal? I am not. I want to have it that way. That's all." She turned to the waiter and ordered two coffees and a piece of pastry.

"The pastry is for Rambabu." She said when the waiter left. The man cast his glance upon the boy briefly and casually asked, "Who is he?"

"Don't you know him?" The woman asked. There was

sadness in her voice.

The man looked intently at the boy and said, "No, I don't."

"Look at him carefully," the woman said. "Of course, he is your son." She gave him the information in an easy manner.

The man drew on the cigarette rather heavily. Now without taking further interest in the boy, he asked, "When did you start smoking?"

"After Mummy's death," the woman replied, exhaling smoke from her mouth.

"Oh! I am sorry. So your Mummy is ..."

"Yes, she is no more." She cut him short with a callous abruptness.

"Now there are only the two of you, you and your father."

"No, there are three of us."

"How far did you go in college?" It was an effort to change the topic and steer clear of the boy.

"Only that far as you know. I asked you to marry me. You couldn't decide. You probably thought that I was a fast girl, not having the desired reputation and if you married me, how would you conduct yourself in the prevailing social structure. I had warned you that I wouldn't kill my child. I decided to bring him into this world and boldly own him as my child. That's what I did. You know that it was at that time that they threw me out of the college."

The man muttered a few inaudible, sympathetic words. "I

am sorry all this happened. You know I had to leave for Madras in rather a hurry."

"Yes, I remember everything. But why are you feeling guilty? I don't blame you for whatever happened. It was my fault, too. Well, forget it."

The man brought out a packet from his pocket. "Coffee is yet to arrive. Have a chewing gum in the meanwhile," he said offering the packet to the woman.

"When did you become a chewing gum addict?" she asked.

"The day I landed in Madras. I become nostalgic when I chew the gum. It reminds me of old times – the days gone by."

The woman made no reply. She took out two pieces from the packet, popped one into her mouth and gave the other to her child . The waiter brought the order.

"Now to tie up the loose ends, tell me what happened after I left?" he said, mixing sugar in the coffee.

"What's there to tell? After they turned me out of the college I went home to live with my parents." She stubbed out the cigarette in the ashtray. "My parents were very angry, but as time passed their fire subsided."

"You didn't marry?"

"No. Who would marry me even if I wanted to ? Then again what about Babu? Mummy was dead and it wasn't possible for Daddy, physially or otherwise, to look after the boy. Yes, my marriage was almost settled, but the man didn't like the idea of Babu living with us.

'Have coffee." He pushed the cup towards her.

She picked up the cup and said, "I would like to ask you a question."

"Please do."

She changed her mind and sipped the coffee silently. He had finished the coffee. He wiped his mouth with his handkerchief and ran his fingers over his moustache.

She asked, "When did you start sporting a moustache?"

"Oh! That ..." He laughed lightly. "Just for fun. I have a friend in the army who sports a moustache. I thought, I would look smart. I grew one like him." He lit another cigarette. "Now tell me, doesn't it enhance my personality?"

"It's all right," The woman said, "I need your advice about something. What kind of education will suit Babu? We have to think about it right away. I mean the profession we would like to put him in."

"Whatever you choose would be the best."

"That's no answer. Do you think you owe him nothing?"

"Why do you repeat the same thing again and again? You are free to bring up the child the way you want to."

They sat silent for a while. Suddenly the woman placed the lit cigarette on the lips of the boy and asked him to inhale. The boy was surprised. Seeing the stern look in his mother's eyes, he held the cigarette in his fingers and drew on it. Coughing ensued and he kept coughing for some time.

"What's all this about?" The man shook his head disapprovingly. "How can you ask a child to smoke?"

"What's wrong with that?" Her eyes emitted a gleam of mischief for an instant and then she presented a grave face.

The man discerned a look of suppressed anger in the woman's eyes. "Nothing wrong with that," he said in a mellow voice. "Don't you think he can do without it? It wasn't good for him, I thought."

"If only I could have found out the difference between good and evil, things wouldn't have come to such a pass. But then, I give a damn. I must live somehow, whatever the circumstances."

The man was getting bored now. However, feigning interest in the subject, he said, "I must tell you something very interesting. That depression in your neck still looks beautiful..."

The woman watched him silently, eyes glued to his face.

"Are you still fond of eating monkey-nuts?" He asked, his eyes devouring hers.

"No. I now detest monkey-nuts. They remind me of the culvert near the cremation ground where I spent so many evenings those days. Please don't mention the monkey-nuts. I have been trying to forget the past. I want to forget everything having the slightest link with the past." She heaved a deep sigh and continued, "Now it's only me and Babu. Nothing else remains – nothing."

The man could sense her sentiments. He said, "Well, I don't see any change in your eyes."

Her eyes had moistened. He panicked and hurriedly called for the bill. He was afraid she might create a scene. She was really getting worked up.

Emerging from the restaurant, they walked a while along the footpath. In the meanwhile, the woman regained her composure.

"Are you married?" She asked him after a brief silence.

"No, not yet."

"There seems to be no need either," she said laughing.

As if caught on the wrong foot, the man surveyed her with a blank expression.

"How long do you think you will be here?" She asked.

"Why do you want to know?"

"No reason. Just by the way."

"Maybe for a month or so."

"Oh!" She said it in a casual manner which had nothing to do with what the man had said.

For a few moments they walked in silence.

"Let's meet again," the man said. "What do you do with your evenings?"

"Nothing." Her voice betrayed remorse. "After you left, everything looked strange and disjointed. I had enough of your 'goodness' don't need more of it."

He winced at her words. She looked at her watch and hailed a taxi." I must be going now," she said. She turned towards the man and said, "Won't you love Babu a little?"

The man looked briefly at the boy in surprise and then stood still.

"Doesn't matter." There was sadness in her voice. "You may not know your mind, but I know mine. I would hate my son to beg for love. I merely wanted to see how you felt about him. Well..." She pushed Babu in the taxi and then climbed in. There were tears in her eyes.

She wiped the tears quickly and turned to Babu. "My son, not a word to Daddy about your smoking a cigarette. I don't know what caused me to do it. I don't know why I behave so queerly sometimes. I really don't know."

A Deer in the Forest

Ambai

Those nights are unforgettable, nights when we listened to stories. It was Thangam Athai who told them. They were not the usual ones about the crow and the fox, the hare and the tortoise. These stories were her own. Some like snatches of poetry, some like never-ending songs, they were without beginnings or ends, unfolding in myriad enticing ways. She would conjure up all kinds of images in our minds. Even *asuras* and *devas* assumed new shapes in her stories. Surpanakai, Tatakai and other such demons were transformed into beings with feelings and emotions. Her Mantarai would bring tears to our eyes. Characters hidden in the dark corners of the epics would be drawn out by Athai's words, much like a bird with broken wings being revived by caressing hands. Was it the magic of night, the expansive central hall of that ancient house, or the closeness of cousins lying next to each other, I do not know, but those stories still reverberate in my mind like the constant hum of a bee.

I see Thangam Athai now in many remembered moments

in that house with its old pillars and its vast central hall. Leaning against the huge wooden door. Carrying the lighted earthen lamp, its flame protected with the loose end of her saree, to set it gently in its niche. Serving food to her husband, Ekambaram. Drawing water at the well, one leg firmly placed against its wall. Manuring the plants.

Dark and beautiful was Thangam Athai – her face smoothed out, with not a trace of wrinkle, her hair silvered over. In Athai's house, there was an old-fashioned harmonium with foot-operated bellows. Only Athai used it. Playing it, she would softly sing a range of songs – from the devotional Thevaram to the love-song *vathaname chandra bimbamo* to the playful *vannan vanthane* – her long, tapering fingers flitting over the reeds of the harmonium like dusky butterflies.

A sense of mystery surrounded Thangam Athai. There was pity in the kind looks others directed at her, in their comforting strokes, their moist eyes. Ekambaram Mama had another wife besides Athai. He treated Thangam Athai as he would a flower. No one ever heard him call her using the all-too-familiar "di." He called her Thangamma. Even so, Athai seemed distant, as if behind a screen of smoke. It was Muthu Mama's daughter, Valli, who solved this mystery – not that what she said made much sense to us. According to Valli's mother, Thangam Athai had never "flowered."

"What does that mean?" many of us asked.

"It means she never came of age." Valli was the one who

had graduated to wearing half-sarees.

"But her hair is all grey?"

"That's different."

After that we began to look closely at Athai's body. We tried to discover what a body which had not flowered would be like. It was not at all clear. When she came out of the bath, wrapped in wet clothes, she appeared no different from any other woman. Nor when she stood in her green saree, the red blouse held by a firm knot under her bosom, her hair gathered into a knot. Valli's mother had once told Valli, "Hers is just a hollow body."

Where was the hollow? Could it be that, like the broken wing of a bird, it was not visible?

One evening, they cut down a huge withered tree in the garden. The final stroke of the axe brought the tree crashing down, with a rush of rustling leaves. When cut open, we saw that its inside was hollow. Valli dug her elbow into my waist and whispered, "There, that's hollowness." This cloven tree, exposing itself so fully that everyone could see the emptiness inside, how could we compare this to Athai's glistening dark body?

What secret did her body keep hidden? How was her body different? Summer afternoons, she would lie down to res. .n the store room. She would place her arm gently round us when we lay down next to her, our heads nestling against her bosom that had been freed from the taut blouse. Enjoying the total security afforded by her bosom, her hips, her arms, we would wonder what was hollow inside her. Her body was warm to the touch. It seemed to be brimming with energy, like a fruit laden with juice, and its regenerating vitality lashed over us many a time like a surging river – when she touched us, caressed us or, with a firm hand, massaged oil into our bodies. The cow yielded milk only at her touch. Seeds she sowed invariably sprouted.

Amma said she had a lucky touch. When my little sister was born, Athai had come down to stay with us. "Akka, stay close to me, keep touching me. Only then will I not feel the pain," Amma moaned as we were being sent out of the room. When we inched back to the door and looked again, Thangam Athai was gently stroking Amma's bulging stomach, saying in a soft voice, "Don't panic. Nothing will go wrong."

"Oh Akka! If only you too ..." Amma sobbed.

"Come on, what is it that I lack? I live like a queen, my house is full of kids," said Athai. Ekambaram Mama's second wife had seven children.

"Your body cannot ..." Amma choked on another sob, unable to complete her sentence.

"Why, what's wrong with my body?" Athai asked. "Isn't my appetite normal? Don't I sleep well? This body too is like all other bodies. When hit, it feels the pain, blood clots. When a wound festers, pus drips. Food gets digested. What else does one want?"

Amma took Athai's hand and pressed it to her cheek. "Oh! How they wounded and gored your body ..." Amma wailed, still holding Athai's hand.

Valli's mother had told her that there was no medicine that had not been tried on Athai's body. She was sure to receive the preparation of every *vaidyan* visiting the town. Athai was given English medicines aiso. Sometimes, after taking certain medicines, she would sleep as if for ever. They even offered ritual worship with neem leaves and rattle drum. In the hope that a sudden fright would help, they had a dark, shrouded figure jump on Athai when she went into the backyard one late evening. Athai fell down shrieking, and knocked her head against the granite stone used for washing clothes. She still has the scar at one end of her forehead. When the next *vaidyan* arrived, Athai, it seems, cried out, "Leave me alone, please leave me alone." When they went to arrange a second wife for Ekambaram Mama, that night Athai ground the seeds of the *arali* flower and drank the potion. They somehow managed to save her by giving her an antidote. And Mama said, his eyes brimming with tears, "I don't want anything that would hurt you." After that, Athai herself selected a girl for him. That was how Sangamalam came into the family. All this, of course, was information garnered by Valli.

Without releasing her hand from Amma's hold, Athai was stroking her head with the other, murmuring, "Forget, forget everything. Why do you rake up my story when you are about to deliver?"

That night, my little sister was born.

It was later, during one of my visits home, that Athai narrated this story.

It was the rainy season. One night ... A jamakalam had been spread at one end of the hall and a few pillows set out. Some pillows had cases soiled with hair oil. Some were without cases, made of thick darkish cloth and stuffed with cotton that had grown lumpy. They were not pillows that were in daily use. These were given to us children when there were guests. Children who had played all day long, eaten their fill and who fell asleep the moment their heads touched the pillows – would such children even notice minor discomforts?

We heard the noise of the kitchen being cleaned. Then the metallic clang of the bronze vessel, the screech of a door opening, the thud of a sodden broom being placed behind the door. Then, the tin of *kolam* powder grated against cement – the earthen stove must now be getting a *kolam*. Closing the kitchen door, Athai should be coming through the hall.

None of us was asleep. We waited.

When Athai came closer, it was Somu who spoke.

"Athai, tell us a story ... please, Athai."

"So, you are still awake, all of you?"

She stood for a moment, looking at us, then came over and sat down. Kamatchi and Somu crept towards her and, settling their heads on her thighs, looked up expectantly. The others leaned forward on elbows rested firmly upon the pillows.

Athai was tired. Sweat glistened on her forehead. She closed her eyes and thought for a while.

"It was a big forest ..." so she began.

"All the animals lived happily in that forest. There were many fruit-bearing trees there. A rivulet ran on one side. When thirsty, the animals would go there to drink water. Everything the animals needed was available right there. There was no fear of hunters in that forest. The beasts roamed about without the least fear of an unexpected arrow piercing them, threatening their lives. Not that there were no forest fires here, or strangers coming to fell trees, pluck fruits, shoot birds, or hunt the fleeing pig. Yet, it was a familiar place for the beasts and birds dwelling there. They knew on which tree the owl would sit, and how it would hoot when the forest lay wrapped in the silence of night, on which stone the frog would squat and when it would suddenly give a gurgle-throated croak, or where the peacock would dance.

"One day it came to pass that a herd of deer went for a drink of water. Coming away from the stream, one young deer lost its way. Suddenly it found itself in a different forest. A forest with no paths. Where all the trees bore the marks of arrows. There was a waterfall there too, one that tumbled and roared. The forest looked desolate to the little deer, as if it was a deserted, friendless place. The deer trembled. It ran here and there in panic, crying all the while. Night set in. The deer could not live with its fear. The sound of the cataract frightened it. At a distance, a hunter had made a fire, and was roasting the game he had killed. The deer noticed the sparks of the fire. Stealthily, it wandered round and round the forest till, exhausted, it sat down.

"Many days went by. One full moon night, the deer saw that the cataract had gilded itself with moonlight and seemed transformed. Its appearance no longer caused terror. The moonlight fell softly, on everything and as if touched by a magic wand, the deer shed all fear. It liked the forest. Every nook and cranny of the forest became clear to it.

Though a different forest altogether, this too has everything, the deer thought. There's the waterfall. And there the trees, the plants. Gradually the deer was able to see the animals and the birds, the beehive hanging from a tree, the grass shot with green. This new forest no longer held any secrets for the deer, and it roamed everywhere. With all fear gone, the deer became calm."

Athai finished the story. Only the part of the hall we were in was lighted. The rest was in darkness. Imagining the dark spaces to be the forest, we had listened to the story. We had made friends with the deer and in the end we too were at peace. Everyone fell asleep, hugging pillows. Drowsy, resting on the coarse blue, yellow and black pillow, I looked up. And there, still sitting in our midst, arms thrown across her bosom, palms clasping her shoulders and head resting against her knees, was Thangam Athai.

Liberation

Sujata

Venkatrao! When you suddenly declared this morning that I was absolutely inactive, that it was no longer possible for you to lead a life with an inert thing like me, you can't imagine how ecstatic I was Believe me, I couldn't control my laughter at seeing my father who was eating his breakfast, my mother who was serving you all, and my brother who was trying to make you eat more by "entertaining" you with news, all stunned like pictures nailed on the wall. It was not possible for me to hide my feelings and expression however much I tried. When an uncontrollable happiness lit my face, when I laughed heartily, my poor mother was stupefied.

The thought of my heart being deeply hurt, of my mind being blunted by unbearable anxiety and worry made me laugh hysterically, and the thought of having tried to prove all this to you and of having tried to plead with you to take pity on me made me laugh even more. Though it was not possible for me to imagine birds in flight and flowing streams as in a movie, I admit that I did experience such a feeling.

How do they know that the whole drama was really over last night, that I had signed the papers you wanted, and that you would bring your new bride home tomorrow itself.

Just a while ago your friend, whom you abuse as one who ogles me like a nasty fellow, one who hogs my useless preparations with his stupid praises – that friend telephoned. I believe the New Year was spent very happily at our place. He asked me to tell you that your other friends too felt the same. Why wouldn't they be happy? The snacks, the *pulaos* the *biryanis* I made after slogging all day like an ox, the arrangements I made using my "degree" brains, the special attention I paid to your drinks party by frying cashew nuts – aren't these all "colourful?"

The Parimala you introduced to me that day is "colourful" too! How can I deny it poor thing, the kitchen isn't hers as yet. When the mother or sister-in-law looks after the house, she happily gets ready, wears an uncrumpled organdy saree and a smile on her lips – "she is very colourful." Venkatrao, what liveliness can you find in a person like me with tired eyes, with no energy even to have a bath?

When Parimala enquired of me, "How come you look so dull Mrs.Rao?" I too laughed (with Parimala) at these "cheap" jokes you cracked: "She's like that , a touch-me-not, she doesn't like people, she doesn't belong to our world." What's your world, Venkatrao, you who can't think of anything other than yourself? What do you know about me – that you could tell

Parimala that there is no trace of any enthusiasm in me, that I don't possess normal qualities like love and happiness, that you have missed a lot? I am sure I heard you say all this.

"Even now we are strangers, Parimala," you said in a voice filled with false emotion. True. It is cent percent true. Your heart-rending anxiety that I don't read books, that I don't attend literary discussions, that I don't respond to poetry, is true. Very true. When, have you really known me? Your habits, your food, your tastes, an inventory of your likes, you have listed them one by one. I learnt from your mother how they brought you up with a lot of love and special care. I have taken the burden off her shoulders on to mine (at least, she is relieved of the burden of you), your food, ironing, bath, bed – all these! All these I have organised with more interest than my own things. When you took all this I supplied tea when you had discussions with your friends. I swept all your cigarette and my dowry, did you care to ask me at least once about my needs, Venkatrao?

I had supplied tea when you had discussions with your friends. I swept all your cigarette butts away. When someone came to see the great person that you are, I hid behind the door and gave them information. You shouted for coffee, but did you ever ask me to take part in the conversation? How would you know me? I love to watch the morning sun rays piercing the darkness. You don't get up till eight, By the time you get up, hot water for your shave with your breakfast must be ready. So where do I get to see the sunrise, except to wash dishes with a sleepy face? I enjoy sitting out in the moonlight and chatting. But the moment you see the moonlight and bed, without letting me utter another word, you like to roll over me and within minutes "relax" in sleep. When it is raining, when each drop trickles down quietly from tree tops, I love to interpret each droplet. But as soon as you see a drop of rain, you think it would be lovely to eat *pakodas* and *bajjis*. By the time I get them ready for you to eat, the rain I had wished to watch would have poured and stopped. I couldn't tell you any of this.

You said I didn't know how to laugh. True. Where do I have the time to smile at you with the endless, back-breaking work? As you couldn't tolerate the child's cry or noise on your return from work you had "ruled" that I should put the child to sleep by the time you came back. I was troubled day and night trying to keep the child awake during the day and putting it to sleep just as you came in. So where did I have the patience to take the jasmines you brought and feel happy? Our understanding of each other stopped there. I am not too worried though. In fact, I wanted to express my gratitude to you – you have left, that's enough. I have only to look mournful for a couple of days. After that, endless rest. I have received the entire household's sympathy and affection because of your having kindly broken away from me. I am happy that my *avatar* as the wife of a genius has come to an end. Nobody will find fault with my work hereafter. I am even happier that I don't have to tolerate your anger nor listen to your boasts.

It may take a while for me to end my role as Venkatrao's wife and realise who I am and what my nature is, but that's all right. The wings you had clipped will sprout slowly. After putting the horrible past lived with you behind me, no matter whether I get back to my lost studies, or make a living by making *appalams,* I know that only golden days are ahead. For having given me those days, once again, with gratitude...

Once upon a time, the slave at your feet.

The Profession

Ismat Chughtai

I was aware that she was a courtesan. That dyed red hair, those tight outfits and the crowd of men all the time. Music, dance, shrill and heavy laughter. These made me reel in my room without any reason. We women could defeat many a heavyweight, but an encounter with a courtesan and there goes all our femininity. This is the main reason that a mother while singing a lullaby to her child always emphasises that a courtesan is a serpent, dragon and heaven knows what else!

And this childhood abhorrence of the courtesan, seems to have entered my blood stream. Let a thousand women cross my path I couldn't care, but the smell of a courtesan would make me alert like a targeted deer. I remembered that I happened to smell them first in my childhood. At Bahraich at the sacred tomb of Sayyad Mian, every Thursday there used to be a gathering of the courtesans from all over the place. On those auspicious days pious and noble souls would also throng the tomb in larger than usual numbers. I don't know why one day a veteran courtesan picked me up in her arms. Oh her silken slippery dress and that peculiar aroma from her breast! Immediately I climbed down from her arms.

That day everyone teased me at home that a prostitute had touched this poor me. I felt such deep resentment that I kept on crying for a long time. Then one day an aunt of mine visited us. She kissed me and there it was, the same slippery dress and aromatic breast! I don't know why but I escaped from her! My guess was correct. My colourful aunt did not stay for more than a month. My Abba Jan, a father of ten, fell for her head over heels. My poor mother, she just shrivelled. It was like a dull betel nut shop finding it difficult to survivc in front of a gorgeous restaurant! Poor mother had to find recourse in black magic. And then only did my aunt complain of a pain in her liver and suddenly leave. My point is that we women have a sixth sense to detect a courtesan. As it had been said their armouries force us to erect defensive walls! She was coming down and I was going up when I smelled her. O God where had I come? What would the world say? What impression would my department have about me? Especially when it was a conglomoration of frustrated people. These departmental bureaucrats have little trouble outdoing the proverbial village gossips.

It was the day of Id. What is Id or what is Muharram for a person in my kind of poverty! Still in bed, unchanged I just kept reading the newspaper. Pots and pans and crockery were making a noise in the neighbour's apartment since four in the morning. These poor souls are very concerned about religious offerings and prayers. As I was having my breakfast, someone knocked on my door, and burst into the room before I could compose myself.

No one can be certain of the consequences when a courtesan forces herself in like that. It was such an alarming experience that I got quite confused.

"Oh no! I hope you haven't finished your breakfast! – Delicious *sewaian* has been cooked," she hissed from her tight outfit. Stupid thing! She didn't even know that the days for such tight outfits had long passed for her. She looked like dough tied up in shoe laces.

"I don't eat sweets in the morning," I said like a proud housewife.

"Really! Not even on Id? Please taste it just for my sake!" She sat down on my bed without any formality.

Oh my God! I hope she has not taken me for a courtesan and come to wash my sins with those sacred offerings. How could I explain that I was pure, chaste and noble. She must have repeated such requests to thousands of her lovers! I was furious. but when she kept on insisting without any shame – I took two spoonfuls.

"My cook said that you are a Muslim. Ever since then I have been looking forward to meeting you, but you are not to be found during the day." Then someone called her and she disappeared as suddenly as she had come.

I took two more spoonfuls! Oh God, I really felt like putting my fingers in my mouth and forcing myself to vomit. What had happened to me, that I should be eating from a prostitute's earnings? The detestable money, earned through selling her body. The money of a degraded and fallen woman!!

Then all sorts of shameful and subservient thoughts started to come to my mind. The money of this prostitute is also the money of my ancestors. I had an uncle who spent Rs 30,000 in only three weeks on such a prostitute. I don't care if one of them was my aunt –or related to this red haired woman. I started to eat the *sewaian* with more relish as if I was collecting all that thrown-away wealth. I felt contented. At least I was making a rich person somewhat poor. I took another spoonful and my mouth was filled with dried fruits and rose water, a pistachio came between my teeth. Greasy little bubbles started to dance in my mouth as if I had chewed a big fat money-lender, but then the very thought of his abundant fat made me sick. I felt the satisfaction of an anarchist burning British clothes. Our eyes derive immense satisfaction from creating figures of our fancy to fit empty dresses.

I took out Matriculation examination papers from the drawer of my bedside table and started to examine them. Here goes the Id! I still had to examine three hundred more scripts. But when my thoughts wandered, I found it difficult to harness them! I failed a few unfortunate ones. Then threw aside the papers and started to stretch myself. The weather in Bombay is peculiar. One feels as if one is wrapped in a big wet towel. Tired and sleepy, my body getting heavier as if someone had put glue on it and let it dry, I felt myself getting strangely intoxicated. And then a sudden blast of laughter from the neighbour. How unfortunate! I started to pity the poor neighbour. It is possible that the poor thing was forced to sell her treasured chastity. Perhaps a tyrant might have robbed her of her virginity, leaving her no option but to become a bazaar commodity. I felt a sudden affection for her. When as children we fought over food, Amma would throw the food basket at us in disgust and say, "Here you wretched, eternally starved lot! Now go and eat and die!!"

But as always evil thoughts crept into my mind along with noble ones. And as always, as soon as noble thoughts dozed off, evil raised its fangs. Almost against my better judgement, I felt certain that she had became a prostitute by choice. Out of sheer laziness she escaped from the real world and adopted this profession. This neighbour was certainly not made for noble work like sewing or grinding wheat! Normal life has quite a few problems – husband, wife, children, mothers-in-law, sisters-in-law, you and me – the full catastrophe. Who in his or her right mind would want to get involved? She could hardly maintain her youth if she had a few mothers-in-law and sisters-in-law! How convenient!

One day as soon as I entered my apartment, screaming and

shouting greeted me from the neighbour's room. A tiring and exhausting day, but one could not hope for peace here. After school one needs total relaxation for a few hours to recover one's strength! It seemed that the students squeeze the brains of teachers as if they chew it before spitting it out like sugarcane. It is not easy to bring freshness into the sucked out sugarcane and face the same sharp gnawing teeth next morning! The same routine for 260 days in a year, the same fate of the sucked sugarcane.

The door opened and she entered, her heels click-clacking noisily on the floor.

"I am tired of this Nigar – only Allah knows why there is so much fuss over this wretched school work, as if hell has broken loose!" How times have changed! Even the daughters of a prostitute show so much sensitivity to education and homework. She even has the audacity to be critical in these matters!

"Then why do you send her to school – withdraw her."

"Oh no! withdraw her? What advice – who ever would care for an uneducated girl. Now everyone wants a girl fluent in English like a Mem Sahib."

A new revelation – one has to be educated even in this profession – probably has to quote Shakespeare and Wordsworth! "What really has happened?"

"I only said darling Nigar please wear that 'khara payjama'* – but no – always no – only those European dresses –"

"She might listen to you if you persuade her – actually some people are coming from Delhi." She confided to me and I felt like scratching her red beetroot-like face – So? I should persuade her? So in my B.T. I was taught to give professional advice to a prostitute's daughter. Just imagine me teaching such girls to wear 'payjama' for the people of Delhi, sari for Calcuttans and shalwar for Lahoris. How wonderful! Moreover the name – Nigar-Malti- I never liked such motivation. What is this? Is this a symbol of Hindu- Muslim unity or an example of Hindu-Muslim friction? Renowned leaders had lost the battle to solve this problem and here was this lady whose so-called open mindedness had muddled all this Hindu-Muslim issue. But it is my way to consider everyone helpless. Perhaps this red-haired Sethani was forced into this situation of helplessness – and could not remember in her muddle-headedness whose gift was this Nigar, and instead of depriving someone of their right she cared for both of them. Anyway!"

"Why don't you come to our place sometime? – " she said with stubbornness – and before I gave her a rude reply, she said – "Nigar has learned new techniques of dance."

I really love a prostitute when she is dancing. She exactly resembles a hardworking labourer who for the sake of his living is tied like a bull to the yoke of capitalism, or a housewife grinding the mill. Dancing is no joke, each piece of flesh in the body is well shaken, as if one has ground ten seers of wheat. I do not detest the darker side of a prostitute's life because she is a bit different, no, not at all – but – no it is unnecessarily difficult to explain no not even this – but just the same.

I plucked up courage and went to Sethani's apartment the next day, just to see how their home looked from inside. Oh my! Just imagine the house of a small Raja or a minister – large portraits – statues of naked women – these courtesans, I wonder why they keep the portraits of naked women in their houses – what is the use of this – perhaps the Sethani wants to hide her horrible wrinkles in the shadow of these perfectly formed statues – must be their special technique! Nigar was really bashful to see me as if she had just been hatched from an egg, and came to me after a great deal of coquetry. When the Sethani showed her displeasure, she put on a record on the gramophone and began to dance.

These prostitutes! Oh my God! I was informed that their bodies decay and rot, but the Sethani was solid like a steel monument, and her offspring God forbid –what a supple and active body, as if a serpent was stretching herself. When putting one wrist on the other, she makes a knot and hits the earth with her tiny toes so that the whole world seems to swing with her. My heart suddenly started to beat faster. Oh this serpent, who knows how many will be bitten by her; who knows how many victims she will put in her hunting bag. A woman is usually jealous of other women for no reason, but God save us all from a prostitute! A woman gets her share, that is a man from the market and then moves on, but no escape from a prostitute. Ordinary people take their groceries according to their needs from the shop and then go away, but special people hoard sacks and sacks of grain in the heart of their basement – result? If you have studied economics then you would know the result – dearth of food! This struggle which is going on with these prostitutes is like the struggle of workers with the capitalists. One works hard and the other reaps the benefit. It is said that finally a burning day would come when the workers would crush the capitalists and would take away all their wealth. Perhaps women would one day attack and take away the "capital' of these prostitutes. Perhaps!!

Came evening and the customers started to come – I was sitting in a corner shame- faced and was looking for an excuse to take flight so that they did not take me for one of them. And finally it happened. She fixed me up with a dim editor. I could not even protest and she sold me off!

Soon the hall was full – colourful women and debauched men – they started to laugh loudly. In one corner a few started to drink and gamble. In another corner Nigar, surrounded by men, was laughing and showing off! She was the centre of attraction. One middle-aged man was trying to pull her into his lap, and she was hitting him coquettishly and laughing.

But the Sethani really was worth looking at. Wearing a deep coloured, gaudy dress which looked drab in the daylight, but was sparkling now. Equipped with her make up she was looking like a new bride of four days and, surrounded by young men, she was demurely coquettish. She was looking so young and so beautiful. I was sitting there stunned and wondering about the secret of youth – coquettishness or tender years?

And there that confounded editor was chewing me. Progressive and clever talk, and with such charm that I could only stammer in confusion. His full attention was on those nude paintings which were hung near me – but I started to imagine that perhaps they were stuck on my body. Continuously touching those pictures with his fingers he was trying to explain their finer points. My reply was sheer embarrassment and looking for something important in my purse. Somehow he would come back to the serious problem of a woman's breast, and creating romance in his watery eyes he was making suggestive moulds with his bony hands and explaining all this to me. Though I am quite obstinate, even I was forced to fix my eyes on the pattern of the rug a few times. His every movement seemed to indicate that he was kneading my body like flour with his feet then, after making a horrible image, destroying it. He was really enjoying squeezing me like that and was smiling continuously. With bitterness I felt like making fun of a particular part of his body in such a way that even his dirty smiling eyes for once blinked with shame. But my civility kept me in check!!

At the first opportunity I ran towards my room. I saw an officer near the gallery munching Nigar with gusto and she was crooning and scratching him.

In bed I could neither sleep, nor do anything. The inspectress was visiting the school next day. To attract her attention, I had to woo her with many tricks: the lesson must be effective, my conversation impressive, dress dignified and my manners mild but firm – an attentive class, correct use of the black board – emphasis on the importance of the analytical method of teaching – these were special tricks of my respectable profession! While lying down I started to do physical exercises – and then suddenly the thought flashed through my mind, that if someone saw me in this situation – the very thought of someone's presence made me so lonely. How lonely I was, except for the company of the laughter, which was tumbling like huge rocks from the Sethani's apartment and hitting my brain. The jingling of bells and the sounds of clapping started to creep into my body and started to vibrate my nerves – and then evil thoughts started to toss and turn in my mind.

If anyone had an inkling of those thoughts – heaven knows what would happen. I often shudder with fear at such thoughts. For example, I felt that this Sethani was trying to please her customers with her attire and make up only for the sake of a living – I do the same: respectably dressed, mentally prepared I go to the court of my customers. The only difference is that all my wisdom and intellect are dried and sucked sugarcane – and the Sethani – a pitcher full of juice – I sell my brain, and the Sethani her body! And the value of my brain is equal to a secondhand tyre, that is Rs 70, and the Sethani earns the same amount in her one sweet yawning! Even my father who was a prominent officer in His Majesty's India Services could not earn as much in his whole lifetime! We are both sitting in the bazaar to sell our commodities. Different goods, but the goal is the same! The position of my sucked up brain in front of her pneumatic body is like a small *paan* and *bidi* shop in front of a cricket club. I am certainly beaten in this business. And then I started to burn in the fire of my own imagination. People do sympathise with the courtesans and want to improve their lot – certainly not that they should completely disappear – no, but those who were in a bad condition, they should live a better life! – their dirty clothes turn into glamorous ones – the homes which are located near dirty sewers, should move to "Marine Drive". The customers should come but not in such large numbers that they feel sick and tired. But here for us even if our salary and grades go down every year no one would give a hoot – students – or in other words Hell's caretakers – their number might double, headmistresses suck you dry, office clerks chew you up, committee members swallow you up and belch – no one would care! Lady teachers are building up the minds of the children and the courtesans are consoling the hearts of the orphans! Both are doing their jobs – then – then why it is so?

Spending the night on such unsavoury thoughts there was little chance to be flirtatious and charming in front of the inspectress. The result was that all hopes of becoming permanent this year were dashed to the ground! The desire to lead a life of contentment ended! And this punishment for one who decided to sacrifice her life for the sake of the nation ... that ... but the nation was sick of these half –dead cows – these sick goats – their very sight evokes the repulsion of the nation!

Next day the Sethani came again – and started to give me advice in such a way as if I was one of their real neighbours, spending my life without much thought and care.

"My God! Study, study, study all the time – the poor wretched brain must have been numbed!!"

I protested meekly.

"See how pale you look – "She started to sympathise with me and in me the ghost of rebellion started to dance – why was she bothering me unnecessarily? O God, where have I come? The building seems to be the dwelling of respectable people – The name plates have respectable names too – Miss Cotino, Miss Walker – Mrs. Abdullah – Miss Rasheed – Mrs...

"That Mr. Hameed wanted to meet you again – " This was the same editor -! So she had decided to take me under her wing in her profession. That is, from her customers she would select the dead and dried on and pass them on to me.

"No I must take you to the cinema today – " she said coquettishly.

"But I have ... " It should be known that my profession is not only respectable but also demanding.

"Oh leave it for once, you are always busy. Mr. Hameed has specially brought this cinema pass for you, and you are trying to avoid it – this is really the age to enjoy life – "

O my God – so this is the end of my respectable profession and the beginning of the profession of "fun and games"!!? – God forbid if my poor mother comes to know about it how would she feel about her virtuous daughter being waylaid, and nearly sold: today cinema passes were coming, tomorrow a Banarsi sari, day after tomorrow diamond earrings, and day after he himself with all his artistic thoughts – and his rough and dried hands making the moulds... O God!

I rudely refused and she left mumbling quite disappointed.

"What was wrong with it? That is why it is said that girls should not go for higher studies."

"Oh yes! And why not? What they will do after education – God save your lovely profession, what is the use of racking your brain? I could not understand why in spite of my rudeness the neighbour kept coming to see me!

I started to rearrange my test papers. Oh God – these failed morons deliberately give so much heartache. I wished that if there was any number lower than zero I could give it to them. Let them go to hell – felt like failing even those who did not fail – so that all of them, like the Sethani, fall on the cave of disaster.

Then another thought came to my mind – no – that wouldn't be a suitable punishment – it was better that I should make them hardworking and courageous lady teachers – so that ... so that – they would ...

I could not think any further.

The Sethani and Nigar went out giggling and laughing with Hameed Sahib and a few other committed admirers to the cinema. I was still awake when they returned. Whenever I started to doze all the evil dragons charged me with their gnawing teeth. How can one work like this? It would be disastrous if I lived for another day or two in this prostitute's neighbourhood. My thoughts were getting mixed up every day. I was too scared even to talk to my conscience – God knows what comment it might make.

Holding my head in my hands, I kept sitting on my bed for a long time. Tired and exhausted the Sethani was sleeping – the apartment was quiet. Some naughty thoughts raised their heads – gave them a little latitude and there was a flood of them – My mind was bubbling with laughter, but there was no smile on my face – Respectability, chastity – keep these rotten eggs under the feather of a hen – what would come out of them ? Not a peacock ! But the irony is that no one gives credit for hatching those rotten eggs – the nation does not give a hoot – that a Devi was carrying the basket of purity. Felt like throwing that basket right in the middle of the street that every pedestrian would completely be covered with that filth. What was happening to me? All this was happening to me because of the neighbourhood of this prostitute! I suddenly remembered my friend Beena! Oh how lovely and beautiful she was! She kept on teaching for nine years – and then one day in panic married an old man – she used to say that she fell in love with him, because of his work for the nation. He spent sixteen years in prison and once upon a time he was quite handsome too. But I knew that Beena was pretending to take shelter under such thoughts such as sacrifices for the nation, just like the Sethani uses nude pictures for her own protection. The truth is that when one is hungry even a solid piece of wood tastes like a *papad.*

I finally resolved to change my flat, otherwise this rare jewel would sink in filth, and that precious treasure for which a woman of the east gives her life would mix in the dirt. In this world a woman's chastity is the only commodity which she sometimes squanders for a living and sometimes gives her life to save; that trump card which she produces at every crisis!!

Exhausted in my confused thoughts, I tried to fall sleep.

Next morning when I was going out the Sethani was arguing with a fruit seller. When she saw me she turned her face like a stranger. My head was high with pride. At least she realised that I was respectable – and she a commodity of the market!

A few days after this incident my cousin and his wife visited me. Since I took the flat I was scared that he would be very angry to know that I lived in such a neighbourhood. As soon as he arrived, laughter came tumbling down like huge rocks from the Sethani's apartment – I shut the door with contempt.

"Continuous nuisance all the time –"

"Where?"

"Up there – a wretched courtesan lives there – unending crowd all the time."

"Courtesan? Here? But that was Nigar's voice –" He said in surprise.

"Oh – So you know them -?" I gave his wife a meaningful glance.

"Oh yes – Haven't you met them yet? I operated on Nigar's tonsils – they come from a reputable family –"

"This – this – the Sethani –"

"Yes dear – wife of Seth Abdullah – they belong to Sir Abdul Karim's family. His wife is from Delhi – belonging to the Chistia family – and – she is Razia's aunt. "

"No maternal aunt – " Razia said.

And I started to hide my confusion in that admonishing earthquake. I was stunned as if I had kicked a holy book. And penitence? Penitence was beyond me.

"It must be – must be – some other apartment – " I stammered.

Contributors

Indira Goswami (Mamoni Raison Goswami) has written more than five hundred short stories and twenty novels. Her stories have been translated into many Indian languages including English. She has received several awards including the Sahitya Akademi Award (1983), the Assam Sahitya Sabha Award (1988), the Bharat Nirman Award (1989) and the Sahardaya Sanman (1992). She has done a comparative study of Madhava Kandal's Assamese *Ramayana*, and Tulsi Das' *Ramcharit Manas* for her Ph.D. She serves as a Reader in the Department of Modern Indian Languages, Delhi University.

M Asaduddin teaches English literature at Jamia Millia Islamia; writes on Bangla and Urdu fiction and translates from Assamese, Bangla, Hindi, Urdu and French into English.

Indira Goswami observes:

"The story came into my mind when I visited Kaziranga wildlife sanctuary with one of my colleagues in the university. We passed through some villages also. Memories rushed back to me and I imagined my childhood in the village of Kamrupa and the prosperity that existed at that time. Only a skeleton of those old times have survived, and everything is as if covered in ashes. I felt this deeply when I went into a small tea shop where a very old couple served us ... I was struck by the degradation of human values which had affected some of the interior villages and towns of Assam, and the human suffering of those who still tried to stick to the old values and traditions. The story thus emerged from the accumulated sorrow of my heart."

Mahasweta Devi (b. 1926) is one of our foremost literary personalities, a prolific and best-selling author in Bengali of short fiction and novels; a deeply political social activist who has been working with and for tribals and marginalised communities like the landless labourers of eastern India for years; the editor of a quarterly, *Bortika*, in which the tribals and marginalised peoples themselves document grassroot level issues and trends; and a socio-political commentator whose articles have appeared regularly in *The Economic and Political Weekly, Frontier* and other journals.

Mahasweta Devi has made important contributions to literary and cultural studies in this country. Her empirical research into oral history as it lives in the cultures and memories of tribal communities was a first of its kind. Her powerful, haunting tales of exploitation and struggle have been seen as rich sites of feminist discourse by leading scholars. Her innovative use of language has expanded the conventional borders of Bengali literary expression. Standing as she does at the intersection of vital contemporary questions of politics, gender and class, she is a significant figure in the field of socially committed literature.

The late **Rameshwari Singh 'Kashyap'** was a well-known Bhojpuri poet and dramatist. *Loha Singh* is one of her most famous satirical dramas. It has a legendary place in the field of Bhojpuri literature.

Ashutosh K. Jha writes reports, features and book reviews for leading newspapers. Also publishes articles in Hindi in leading magazines. Translates from Hindi and Maithili into English.

Himanshi Shelat. Gujarati writer. M.A. (Guj. Univ.); Ph.D. (South Guj. Univ.). *b.* January 8, 1947, Surat Gujarat. Retd Lecturer in Eng., presently freelance writing. *A &P.* recd Sahitya Akademi Award, 96; Dhumketu Paritoshik, 95; Umashankar Joshi Award, 95; Guj. Sahitya Parishad Award, 88 and 95. *mt.* Gujarati *Pubs.* 5. *Antaral,* 87; *Ahdheri Galiman Safed Tapkan*, 92 (both short stories); *Paravastavavad,* 87 (crit.); *Pratiroop*, 95 (Makarand Dave's trans. poems, ed.); *Swami Ane Sai,* 93 (letters, ed.).

Rajee Seth, an Indian national, was born in October 1935 in Naushera (now in Pakistan). She has degrees in literature, comparative religion and philosophy. She is a short story writer, novelist, poet, critic and essayist, and has won several prestigious awards for her contribution to Hindi literature. Her work has been translated into several languages and is now prescribed in graduate level courses in many universities. Her first novel *Tat-Sam* (1983) was acclaimed for its extraordinarily rich language and subtle tapestry of human interaction. A more recent novel, *Nishkavach,* has been translated into English (titled *Unarmed*) and published by Macmillan India Limited in 1998. She has also translated into Hindi two collections of Rainer Maria Rilke's letters that focus on the theme of creativity. She was awarded the Residential Fellowship (1996-99) at the Indian

Institute for Advanced Studies, Shimla for Creative Writing. She lives in New Delhi, India with her husband.

P. Lankesh. Kannada writer and film maker. M.A., 59 (in Eng. Lit., Mysore Univ.) *b.* March 8, 1935. Konagavalli, Shimoga Dist., Karnataka. Formerly teaching, presently journalism and freelance writing. *Car.* Lecturer in Eng. Lit, Bangalore Univ., 59-79; Editor, *Lankesh Patrike*, weekly, since 80, *A&P.* recd National Award, 77, for best direction; State Award, for best feature film, 80; Karnataka Sahitya Akademi Award, 87; Book of the Year Award 87; Sahitya Akademi Award, 93; Shivarama Karantha Pratishthana Award, 94, etc. *mt.* Kannada. *Pubs.* 20. *Biruku*, 66; *Mussanjeya Katha-Prasanga*, 78; *Akka* (all novels); *Kereya Niranu Kerege Chelli*, 63; *Kallu Kalaguva Samaya, 91* (both short stories); *Sanskranti*, 72 (play). Has trans. Sophocles and Baudelaire into Kannada. Made four films in Kannada.

Harikrishna Kaul. Kashmiri and Hindi fiction writer. M.A. (Kashmir Univ.); M.Phil (J.N. Univ.) July 22, 1934, Srinagar, J&K. Teaching, retd., now freelance writing. *Car.* Taught Hindi lang. and lit. in different colleges of J&K State; Part-time Lecturer, Kashmir Univ.; Visiting Faculty, J.N. Univ., 91; Mem., Adv. Committ. for Kashmiri N.B.T., etc. *A&P.* J&K Academy of Art, Culture and Languages Award 75-76, 98; Central Hindi Directorate Award, etc. *mt.* Kashmiri, also writes in Hindi. *Pubs.* 10. in Kashmiri: *Pata Laran Parbath, 72; Halas Chhu Rotul, 77; Yath Razdane* (all short stories); *Natuk Kriv*

Band (play); in Hindi: *Is Hamam Mein, 67; Tokri Bhar Dhoop,* 76; *Arthi* (all short stories); *Renu Ki Kahaniyan* (crit.) Writes scripts and screenplays for TV serials and films. Visited West African countries and Egypt.

Stephen Herald Mascarenhas. *Hemacharya.* Konkani and Kannada fiction writer. B.Com. (Mysore Univ.) *b.* January 14, 1957, Mangalore, South Kanara Dist., Karnataka. Service in Muscat, since 93 and writing. *Car.* Editor, *Sankoll,* Konkani mly, 79-80. *A&P.* recd Konkani Bhasha Mandal Award, 81; Konkani Sahitya Samiti Award, Mangalore, 88. *Mt.* Konkani. *Pubs.* 3. *Jeevan Sapna.* 75; *Hemacharyacho Motvyo Katha,* 88 (both short stories); *Baai,* 80 (novel). Lives in Oman and visited Dubai, Abu Dhabi, etc.

Manipadma (1918-86). Maithili novelist. His novels include *Ijot Dai* and *Footpath*; recipient of the Sahitya Akademi Award for *Naika Banjara* 1973.

Paul Zacharia. Malayalam fiction writer. M.A. (Bangalore Univ.). *b.* June 5, 1945, Urulikunnam, Kottayam Dist. Kerala. Consultant, Asianet Television and freelance writing. *A&P.* recd Kerala Sahitya Akademi Award, 79 and Katha Award (twice). *mt.* Malayalam. *Pubs.* 11. *Ambadi,* 69; *Oridathu,* 78; *Oru Nastani Yuvavum Gowli Sastravum,* 83; *Salaam America,* 93 (all short stories); *Bhaskara Pattlelarun Ente Jeevithavum*; *Praise the Lord,* 96 (both novelettes); *Govindam Bhaja Moodhamathe* (essays).

A. J. Thomas (b. 1952). Indian English poet with a collection of poems to his credit; also translates poems and fiction from Malayalam into English and vice versa; recipient of Katha Award and AKMG Prize. He presently works as Assistant Editor, *Indian Literature*.

Vijay Diwan. Playwright, actor, environment activist and translator. Teaches Zoology.

Amitabh. Marathi fiction writer. MSc. (in Electronics, Nagpur Univ.); Ph.D. (in Plasma Physics, Bombay, Univ.). *b.* January 3, 1945, Hinganghat, Wardha, Maha. Service, Sr. Scientific Officer, Govt. of Maharashtra. *A&P.* recd Govt. of Maharashtra Award, 81-82. *mt.* Marathi. *Pubs. 7. Pad,* 80; *Lavata*, 90 (both short stories); *Tingee*, 86 (poetry). Also published books on social topics. Chaired two sessions of Dalit Sahitya Sammelan of Maharashtra.

Rabi Pattnaik (1935-91). Oriya short-story writer; has more than four hundred stories to her credit; recipient of Orissa Sahitya Akademi Award, Sarala Award and Sahitya Akademi Award 1992.

Lal Singh. Punjabi fiction writer, M.A. (in Punjabi, Punjan Univ.); B.Ed. (G.N.D. Univ., Amritsar). *b* April 20, 1940, Jhajjan, Hoshiarpur Dist., Punjab. Teaching, Govt. High School and writing. *Car.* Secretary, Sahit Sabha Mukarian, 77-84; Gen. Secretary, Sahit Sabha, Desuya, 80 onwards; Exec. Mem., Kendri Lekhak Sabha, 78-93. *A&P.* recd Principal Sujjan Singh Award, 96. *Hons.* honoured by Punjabi Lekhak Sabha, Bhogpur, 91; Lok Lekhari Manch, Batala, 93; Punjabi.

Pubs. 4. *Markhory,* 84; *Ballour,* 86; *Dhup-Chhain,* 90; *Kali Mitti,* 96 (all short stories).

Chandra Prakash Deval Rajasthani and Hindi poet. MSc. 73; Ph.D., 87 (in Biochemistry). *B.* August 14, 1949, Gotipa Vill., Udaipur Dist., Raj. Service, Dept. of Biochemistry, J.L.N. Medical College, Ajmer and writing. *Car.* Mem., Gen. Council & Exec. Board, Sahitya Akademi, New Delhi, 1998-2002. *A&P.* recd Sahitya Akademi Award, 79; Bharatiya Bhasha Parishad Award, 92; Kaluram Pediwal Award, 89; Sahitya Akademi Translation Prize, 95, in Rajasthani, etc. *mt.* Rajasthani, also writes in Hindi. *Pubs.* 19. *Paagi, 77; Kavad, 87; Marag,* 92 (all poetry); *Kaal Mein Kurjan* (poetry, trans., from Hindi); in Hindi: *Aartnad, 90; Bolo Madhvi, 95; Smritigandha,* 96 (all poetry). Edited a few anthologies and trans. poetry from Oriya, Hindi and Gujarati.

Ishwar Chander (1937-92). Sindhi short-story writer. He was in the service of Indian Railways; author of more than two hundred and fifty short stories; recipient of the Central Hindi Directorate Award and Rajasthan Sahitya Akademi Award.

Ambai, *nom de plume* of C. S. Lakshmi, is a leading writer in Tamil and researcher in Women's Studies. She is the author of two collections of short stories, and of a critical study, *The Face Behind the Mask: Women in Tamil Literature*. She was a Homi Bhabha Fellow for 1990-92. Tamil fiction writer. M.A. (Bangalore) Ph.D. (J.N. Univ.) *b.* 1994, Tamil Nadu. *Car.* School Teacher; later taught in a college, T.N. *A&P.* recd

Narayanaswamy Aiyar Prize, for fiction. m*t.* Tamil, writes also in Eng. *Pubs.* 4. *Andhi Malai*, 67 (novel); *Siragugal Muriyum, 76* (long story); *Veettin Moolayil Oru Samayalarai*, 88 (short stories).

C. T. Indra teaches English at the University of Madras. She was Senior Fulbright Fellow at Harvard, the British Council Visiting Scholar in UK, and a Research Fellow at the University of California, Santa Barbara. She has served on the Tamil Bhasha Samiti and the Chayan Parishad of the KK Birla Foundation (Delhi) for the Saraswati Samman. Dr. Indra translates short fiction from Tamil into English for journals and newspapers. Her translations won the first prize in the British Council Translation Competition for the South Zone (1988) and the commendation prize in the First Katha Translation Contest in 1994.

C. Sujata (b. 1952) has worked as a journalist for several years. Her novel *Sapta Bhujangalu* has been accredited by NBT as a book worth translating into other Indian languages, she has published several short stories.

M. Shridhar (b. 1962) teaches English at the University of Hyderabad. He translates from Telugu to English and from English to Telugu. He has won the Jyestha Literary Award and Katha Commendation Prize for Translation jointly with Alladi Uma. His other interests include Literary Criticism and Gender Studies.

Ismat Chughtai (b. 1915), one of India's foremost Urdu

writers, published several novesl and collections of short stories. She was known for her committed writing during the Freedom Movement in India when, as part of the struggle, she joined with other writers in forming the Progressive Writers Association, a radical organisation of writers who used their writing to campaign for freedom and equality. Ismat Chughtai joined in campaigns for justice and civil liberties. Her published works include *Choten, Churi Mui, Kaliyan Shaitan* (a collection of short stories) and several novels.